Billionaire and the Beauty

Jane Daly

ISBN-13: 978-1-965352-81-6

Chapter 1

Samantha held the letter in one trembling hand. The brown teddy bear stared at her with black-button eyes. How had he gotten so close without anyone seeing him?

A gift for my best girl.
Love,
Your soon to be not so secret admirer

The writing was scrawled, as if scratched onto the blank sheet in a rush.

Sam dropped the letter like it was on fire. It fluttered to the floor of her dressing room and lay face-up. Menacing. Dangerous.

Her phone chirped with a text.

Her manager.

Skyler: Almost ready for you.

Sam stared at her pale face reflected in the mirror. No way could she go out to the studio as if nothing had happened. She composed a text to Skyler.

I don't feel well. I have to cancel.

Some called Samantha Jensen a diva. But today, she didn't care.

Instead of a response, her manager burst through the dressing room door with a scowl.

"What's going on, Sam? We needed you on the set, like, ten minutes ago."

Samantha leaned out of the canvas chair and plucked the letter from the floor with two fingers.

"Look." She thrust the letter in Skyler's direction.

Skyler's eyes widened and her mouth fell open. "How did he find you?" she whispered.

"I thought you said the police were closing in on him." Sam couldn't help her accusatory tone. "You said you'd take care of it."

Skyler sank onto the uncomfortable sofa with a groan. "That's what they told me. They said they had a line on your crazy stalker." She raised tortured eyes to meet Sam's. "I'm so sorry."

"What am I going to do?"

After weeks of rearranging Samantha's modeling contracts to throw off the stalker, things had been quiet on that front. At last feeling safe, Samantha had fulfilled some of the commitments Skyler had scheduled months ago.

Skyler got to her feet and dropped the letter onto the seat she vacated. "I'll take care of things out there." She flipped a hand toward the door.

This was the Skyler Sam was used to. All business. "I'll make up an excuse. How would you like to come down with Covid? I'll let Dior know you won't be at the runway shoot next week."

"You'll take care of all the details." It wasn't a question. Sam had people to take care of things.

"I'm on it. You need to find a place to hide out. Change your appearance. Go off grid."

Sam let her head drop into her hands. Skyler made it sound simple.

Samantha hadn't left the rental house on Lake Skaneateles for three days. Each time she approached the French doors leading out to the massive wood deck, panic fluttered in her chest. What if her stalker discovered where she was? He could be anywhere, waiting.

As impossible as that seemed, terror still haunted her sleep and held her captive during the day. The summer storm gave her a handy excuse to not venture out. But today, the sun had burned off the mist hovering over the lake and the soft breeze through the windows beckoned her outside.

With one last glance in the oval mirror over the dressing table, Samantha shoved her bare feet into a pair of flip flops and walked out to the living room. Her sister, Lauren had helped dye her blonde locks an insane shade of blue. Sam used a pair of kitchen shears to cut her hair to chin length. The bangs were uneven and hung over her eyebrows. Lauren had picked up the ugliest clothes she could find from the Goodwill store in Hornell before dropping Sam off at the rental.

"You look like a different person," Lauren had told her.

"That's the plan." They'd hugged goodbye and Lauren had driven off to her fiancé's house on Keuka Lake.

Sam snagged the glass of iced tea she'd left sweating on the dining room table and stepped through the French doors and onto the deck. Humidity rose like a sauna from the damp wood. Inhaling, she walked to the railing and looked out over the lake, blue and clear as an aquamarine.

A girl's voice from the deck next door pulled Sam's attention from the lake.

"Why do I have to wear a life jacket?"

From her vantage point, Sam could see down to the house next door to hers. A deck, the twin to her rental, led from the lower floor out onto the lake. A girl and a man faced each other, arguing.

The man's voice stayed low and modulated. "Because the water is cold and when you fall, I want you to be safe."

The girl's voice rose in outrage. "When I fall? You mean if."

"Amanda, I'm not going to stand here and argue with you. Either wear the life jacket or go back in the house."

"You're so mean!"

Sam smiled as the girl stomped her foot. She judged her age at fourteen or fifteen. The drama ended when the girl snatched the life jacket from the deck and shoved her arms through it.

"Last year drowning deaths numbered five percent of kids ages ten through fifteen. I don't want you to be a statistic."

The man, presumably her dad, must have felt Sam's stare. He looked up, shading his eyes with one hand. Sam felt a flush work its way up from neck to forehead. She swiveled in the opposite direction. A few moments later, she heard the splash as the girl pushed off the deck on a paddle board.

Sam sighed. What would it have been like to enjoy the simple pleasure of learning to paddle board instead of posing for photos? Her childhood had been anything but normal. When Sam shot up to six feet at fourteen, Mom had dragged her to a modeling agency where she'd learned to flirt with the camera instead of boys.

Turning back, Sam watched the dad watch his daughter as she struggled to stand on the board and propel herself forward with the long paddle. She wobbled, got her balance, then tipped sideways into the lake.

The dad must have heard Sam's laugh. He tilted his face up to where she stood, shading his eyes again. She felt a flash of alarm and scurried back into the house.

Skyler's voice echoed in her ears.

"Don't attract attention."

Inside, Sam took a moment to calm her breathing. Someone was out there, waiting. To what end? What goes through the mind of a stalker?

Sam shuddered, remembering the incident when she was sixteen. That feeling of helplessness never completely left her memory.

Logan Walters refused to argue with his fourteen-year-old daughter. Her mother might get worn down by Mandy's whining, but Logan was made of sterner stuff. Now that Mandy was living with him full-time, he needed to establish some firm boundaries. In the past, he'd indulged her every whim, hoping to make the most of their short times together.

Two weeks in the summer, a week in the winter, and an occasional weekend when Vivian wanted a break. Now that his ex had flitted off to Italy with her new husband, he was Dad and Mom to his recalcitrant teen. He'd have to try hard to make up for his daughter being abandoned by her mom.

A movement from next door caught his eye. They had a new neighbor in the rental. He squinted up through the blinding sun reflecting off Lake Skaneateles. Definitely female, though it was difficult to tell with her baggy clothing. She better not be a partier like the last group. Renting to a group of college guys had been a colossal mistake.

Logan turned his attention back to his daughter. She sulked while putting on the life jacket and continued to sulk until she turned her back on him and pushed the paddle board onto the water.

Mandy fell with a huge splash and Logan heard laughter from the upper deck next door. Shading his eyes again, he caught the woman covering her mouth as she laughed. As soon as she saw him looking, her face changed, and she dashed into the house.

"Are you okay?" Logan called to Mandy.

Water dripped from Mandy's head and down her face. She held the board with one hand and used the other to sweep hair from her face.

"Fine," she sputtered.

Logan smothered a smile. "I'm going inside to grab my phone."

Mandy hauled herself back onto the board. "No pictures, Dad."

"I promise."

Logan returned a couple minutes later and set his phone and laptop on the glass patio table. He'd be able to get some work done and watch Mandy at the same time. But first, find out who rented his house next door.

He sent a quick email to his virtual assistant.

Contact the management company and find out who rented my house next door. Thanks.

Mandy waved from the paddle board when he glanced over the railing. He leaned back in the deck chair and watched her struggle with the double-sided paddle while he waited for a response from his VA.

"You should try it, Dad," Mandy called.

Logan had to admit, it did look like fun. "Let me change into my trunks, and I will."

Laptop forgotten, Logan retrieved the second paddle board from the rack and laid it at the end of the deck.

"Don't forget your life vest," Mandy yelled with a cheeky grin.

Logan grimaced. He hated wearing the bulky thing. It always bunched at his paunch. Maybe with Mandy here this summer, he'd lose some of the weight he'd gained around his middle.

"Let's race," Mandy called, paddling in the direction of a floating platform several yards out on the lake. Logan's arms burned with the exertion. But it felt good. He spent way too much time sitting behind his computer screen. This summer with his daughter would be good for both of them. But after summer, what then?

Mandy's private school was in New York City. How would he handle his research and take care of a teenager?

That was the billion-dollar question.

Chapter 2

Sam continued to watch the man and the girl through the French doors. She held a packet of Oreo cookies in one hand and used the other to separate the two sides and lick the frosting from the middle.

"This is what I've been missing my whole life."

Mom had never given Sam access to junk food while she was growing up. As a model, she had to maintain a certain weight and body mass index to compete for coveted modeling assignments. The same strict diet carried into adulthood. Sam couldn't afford to gain a half a pound, or she might lose out to someone younger and thinner. The lifespan of a runway model was mercilessly short. Even now at twenty-two, she was nearing the sunset of her career.

Sam wandered to the fridge and pulled out a carton of whole milk to wash the black Oreo gunk from her teeth. Whole milk was another decadence she'd been denied.

Shouts of laughter from outside pulled her back to

the French doors. The man and the girl were both in the water splashing each other with cupped hands. Sam felt like a voyeur watching through the window. Wandering to the sofa, she plopped down and grabbed the remote. Time to binge watch The Great British Baking Show.

Three hours later, Sam struggled to an upright position. Her stomach still rumbled from the sugar. Pulling her cell phone near, she sent a quick text to Skyler.

Any new notes from the stalker?

No dots appeared to indicate Skyler was sending a response. The text showed it was delivered, but Skyler was probably busy with her other clients. What if Skyler dropped her?

Sam's travel down the path of self-doubt and misery was interrupted by an incoming text. Not Skyler, but her sister, Lauren.

Lauren: How's my favorite sister?

Sam smiled. I'm you're only sister

Lauren: That's why you're my favorite.

Five seconds later, Lauren's face appeared on the screen.

"Hi, Lauren. What's up?"

"I'm calling to see how you're doing."

Samantha eyed the crumpled-up Oreo wrapping. "Peachy. I've eaten more Oreos than I ever knew existed, drank a quart of whole milk, and binge-watched your favorite show. I'm regretting every single one of my life choices."

Sam smiled when Lauren's laugh echoed through the speaker.

"Seriously, Sam, how are you doing?"

"Not great," she admitted. "I miss having people around. I miss being needed. I miss the routine." *And I feel ugly.*

"What can I do?"

Tears prickled the corners of Sam's eyes. What would she do without her sister? "Nothing. Maybe pray this whole thing is over soon so I can get back to work."

"Are they any closer to finding him?"

"I texted Skyler, but I haven't heard back." Sam slumped further down on the plush sofa. What if it took months to find her stalker? Meanwhile, she'd eat herself into a blimp and never be able to work again.

"I better go," Sam said. "Or I'll be inviting you to my pity party." She disconnected and tossed the phone on the coffee table.

Laughter from outside drew her to the French doors. The father-daughter duo sat hunched together staring at a laptop. An unaccustomed feeling slithered up her spine.

On the outside looking in.

"Dinner is ready, Mr. Logan." The housekeeper

spoke from the sliding glass door.

"Thank you, Carmen."

Logan glanced at his daughter whose face was glued to her cell phone. "Let's eat, Mandy."

"Huh?" Mandy looked up.

"Dinner. Eating. Now." Logan stood and stretched. It had been fun watching YouTube videos with Mandy. Perhaps this long summer wouldn't be as difficult as he imagined.

"What are we having?" Mandy asked.

"I don't know. Let's see what Carmen has prepared."

"Does she know I'm vegetarian?"

Logan grimaced. His favorite meals involved lots of animal protein. Did his ex have anything to do with Mandy's food preferences?

Logan moved to the door. "Let's find out."

Mandy refused to be coaxed into conversation, preferring instead to pick all the pieces of chicken from the stir fry and shove them to one side of her plate.

"You need to eat some protein. You should be eating forty-six grams of protein a day at your age."

Mandy didn't look up.

"Did you hear me?"

"Yeah."

Irritation brought heat to his face. If he'd talked to his dad like that, he would have been backhanded. Dad didn't tolerate disrespect. Logan decided to ignore it. For now. He'd rather not instill fear into Mandy, unlike what he grew up with.

"Is there anything you want to do while we're here at Lake Skaneateles?"

Mandy shrugged. "I dunno. There's probably nothing to do." She shoved back her chair. "I'm going to my room."

Logan sighed, watching Mandy's back as she shuffled from the dining room. He had enough money to buy his daughter anything she wanted. Except happiness.

Carmen entered the dining room and began to clear the table. "Don't worry, Mr. Logan. She is a teenager after all."

Logan sent her a wry smile. "I miss her being a little girl."

"They grow too fast."

Logan retreated to his office and opened his laptop to check the stock market closing. His portfolio had lost a few percentage points, but it didn't overly concern him. Fluctuations were a part of investing.

An alert sounded. A new email.

Dear Alumnus:

Our fifteen-year class reunion is getting closer! Save the date—August 24—6:00– ??

We're currently forming the reunion planning committee. Please respond to this email if you are willing to help.

Sincerely,

Penny Armstrong
Committee Chair

Logan remembered Penny as one of the cheerleaders. One of the girls who never gave him a second glance in school. Her boyfriend was, of course, a football player. One of the guys who relentlessly taunted him because of his huge, black-framed glasses, Goodwill clothes, and ratty shoes.

If they could see him now, their opinion would be different. Since the sale of his invention, he could buy and sell them a dozen times before tomorrow.

Logan deleted the email. He had no interest in seeing what his former classmates were up to. Even though it might be fun to show them who he was now.

Maybe not handsome, but his billionaire status made up for not having looks.

Chapter 3

Sam cracked the front door open and let herself exhale. The Uber Eats driver stood there with her food delivery, tapping one foot.

"Thanks," Sam said, grabbing the bag from his hand.

"No problem," said the middle-aged driver. Sam barely spared him a thought as she closed and locked the door.

"Smells delicious," she said to the empty kitchen. She didn't bother to transfer the Peanut Delight to a plate, instead she snagged a fork and ate from the to-go container.

The combination of rice noodles and spicy sauce brought dopamine flooding into her system. After a few bites, Sam headed to the French doors.

No one sat on the deck next door. Neither father nor daughter were anywhere in sight. Sam stepped onto the wood deck and settled onto a lounge chair with her food.

"Slow down," she cautioned herself. Mom always chided her sister for eating too fast. Mom chided Lauren about a lot of things, including her size. Lauren wasn't overweight per se, merely big-boned. Sam took after their willowy mother, while Lauren resembled their dad's square shape.

The early evening sun created shimmering diamonds on the lake surface. Sam found herself listening to the quiet sounds of the lake readying itself for night. A few birds took flight, their bodies like black specs in the sky.

She dozed.

"Hi."

The voice jarred Samantha from sleep. She straightened in the lounger and grabbed for the empty to-go container before it slid to the deck.

"Uh, hi."

Standing at the top of the stairs was the girl from next door. She wore frayed cutoff jeans and a loose t-shirt reading 'I ♥ NY.' Her feet were bare, and her dark hair swung around her face.

"Are you busy?" Her question was tentative as if she expected to be banished back to her own house.

Sam smiled. At last, another human being to talk to. "No."

The girl took this as an invitation to advance. She sank onto a lounger that was the twin of Sam's. "I'm Mandy. I'm staying with my dad next door." She hooked a thumb over her shoulder.

"I'm S-Vera. Vera Samuels. Everybody calls me Sam." Whew, that was a close one.

"How long are you staying here?"

Sam shrugged. "I'm not sure." A few weeks, a month, longer?

"The last guys who stayed here were huge partiers. My dad rarely let me outside because they kept checking me out." Mandy shuddered. "Gross. They were, like, ancient."

Sam hid a smile behind her hand. Anyone over eighteen was likely 'ancient' to this kid.

"I guess I'm ancient too, then," Sam said.

Mandy laughed. "Probs. Anyway, I'm bored."

"Yeah, me too. Why don't you come over tomorrow, and maybe we can hang out?" Did she sound too desperate?

Mandy shrugged. "I guess."

At that, the girl stood and shuffled to the stairs leading down to the strip of grass separating Sam's house from hers.

As the sun began its descent behind the hill across the lake, the light grew dim and hazy. The air cooled and softened, a telltale sign of dusk approaching. In the distance, muted sounds of late revelers could be heard drifting towards the house, blending with the gentle lapping of the water against the shore. Somewhere in the darkness, a dog barked, its lonely howl echoing through the stillness.

Sam reached into the pocket of her elastic

waistband pants to retrieve her phone. She checked for texts or emails from Skyler but found nothing. A sinking feeling of abandonment washed over her. Without her successful career, what was she? Who was she? Just a has-been, forgotten in the eyes of others.

She knew too well what happened when you were out of the public eye for even a short time. Some of her fellow models had taken time off, only to find it nearly impossible to get a new contract. Sam's publicist was no doubt frothing at the mouth to get her photographed doing something as mundane as eating at a restaurant.

Her world had shrunk to this rental house and a fourteen-year-old girl.

"Don't go out in public," Skyler had warned. If her stalker wasn't caught soon, Sam would likely lose her mind.

Logan read the email from his virtual assistant in New York City.

The house was rented by a modeling agency, Top Notch Talent. It was signed by the CEO, Gaylord McManus, and has been rented for three months. Paid in full.

Logan grimaced. A model lived next door? Just what he needed, another diva. Like Mandy's mom, his ex.

But the woman he'd spied on the deck didn't look like a model. Baggy clothes and blue hair.

Not the typical look of someone who posed in front of a camera for money. Logan shrugged and stepped outside to enjoy a second cup of coffee. Today, he'd find something to occupy his daughter. Her complaints of 'I'm bored' were getting on his last nerve. The community center offered youth programs throughout the summer. He'd convince Mandy she needed to get involved.

The sound of footsteps on the next-door deck floated across to where Logan stood in the morning quiet. Revelers hadn't yet sliced through the pristine lake surface. That noise would come later, after vacationers rose from their sleep-induced hangovers to step blinking into the bright sunlight.

Logan leaned a hip against the deck railing and peered over at the woman mirroring his stance on the deck of his rental. She raised her hand in a tentative wave. Huge sunglasses obscured most of her face and a straw sun hat was pulled low. Logan returned the wave and swung around to face the lake, embarrassed he'd been caught staring.

The sliding door behind him opened, and Mandy appeared at this side, yawning.

"Whatcha doing?" she asked.

Logan put an arm around her, amazed again at how she'd sprouted up in the past six months. Soon she'd be as tall as he was. At his height of five nine, she'd easily surpass him, especially since it looked like Mandy had inherited her mother's height.

"Enjoying the quiet," Logan replied.

Mandy placed both hands on the railing and leaned back. "Hey, there's Sam."

"Who's Sam?"

"Our new neighbor." Mandy pointed in the direction of the woman staring out at Lake Skaneateles.

"How do you know her name?"

Mandy made a disgusted sound. "I went over there last night and met her. She's nice."

Outrage and alarm filled Logan's chest. "You know you're not supposed to talk to strangers."

"Oh, good grief, Dad. Don't go all 'stranger danger' on me. I'm fourteen."

"Fourteen does not exempt you from being careful."

Mandy's eyes rolled in typical teenage fashion. "If you're so concerned, go next door and meet her."

Logan felt a jolt of panic. Sweat tickled his underarms and created a pool of moisture on his palms. "Oh, I don't think so."

Mandy grabbed his arm and pulled him across the wood deck toward the stairs. "Come on, I'll take you." Dropping his arm, she cupped her hands around her mouth and shouted, "Hi, Sam! I'm bringing my dad over to meet you."

The woman jerked around toward them. Her lips formed a straight line. Clearly not excited about Mandy's pronouncement.

Logan let his daughter lead him down the steps, across the grassy berm separating their properties, and up the outside stairs of the next-door deck.

"My dad wants to make sure you're not a serial killer," Mandy said.

Logan felt a warm flush work its way up from chest to neck to cheeks. "I did not—"

"Or a child sex trafficker," Mandy added.

Where did his daughter get such ideas? Probably from her mom.

Logan drew his palm down the leg of his jeans and held out his hand. "I'm Logan Walters."

The woman's hand was soft, and her nails were painted with clear polish and white tips.

"Nice to meet you," she said, withdrawing her hand as quickly as she'd offered it. Probably because his palm was wet.

After noticing the gracefulness of her hands, Logan was surprised that close-up, she towered over him. He was used to having men tower over him. But women, not so much. Mandy's mom, Vivian, was also tall and often wore four-inch heels. Logan was sure she did it intentionally while they were married, just to belittle him. Literally.

"Dad, Sam said she's bored too."

"Are you a model?" Logan wanted to grab his hastily blurted words and shove them back into his mouth. Of course she wasn't a model. Unless she worked for a Goth magazine, she'd never make it with that blue hair and weird haircut.

A ghost of a smile crossed her face. "No. I work in

the industry, though. I'm a … an assistant."

"That's so cool," Mandy said. "I'd love to be a model. But I'm not tall enough. Yet. My mom was a model before she got too old."

Sam laughed. "That happens." She laid a hand on Mandy's shoulder. "Modeling is an extremely difficult career. I have to—I mean, you have to be willing to stand for hours in one position, sometimes in extreme cold wearing something super sheer. Don't even get me started on weight control."

Logan eyed her, suspecting there was more to her story. "You sound like you know a lot about the business."

Sam pressed her lips together and nodded. An awkward moment passed.

"Dad, Sam said I could come over later and hang out. I'm pretty sure she isn't an ax murderer."

"Mandy!" Logan's face warmed with embarrassment. "Sorry. Teenagers," he said by way of apology.

"No worries. I was once a teenager too and prone to say the most outrageous things to get attention."

Unsure of how to respond, he touched Mandy's arm and said, "We'd better get back. Carmen probably has breakfast ready."

Logan and Mandy returned to their own place under the watchful eye of the woman named Sam. He was more determined than ever to find out who the mystery woman was. Why was a modeling assistant renting a very expensive vacation rental on Lake Skaneateles? How did she afford it, and why was her agency covering the cost?

Why did she look like a homeless street person in baggy thrift store clothing?

Something else nagged him. Where had he seen her before? His memory wasn't eidetic, but he had the ability to remember faces—which was invaluable for the software he'd developed and sold to the United States government. For a lot of money.

Who was this mystery woman living in his rental?

Chapter 4

Sam slumped onto the cushioned lounger as soon as Mandy and her dad were out of sight. Skyler's admonition echoed in her ears. "Low profile. Stay out of sight."

Now that she'd—hopefully—convinced the girl's dad she wasn't a threat, Sam wouldn't have to talk to him again. His intense gaze was unsettling. And his palm was yucky damp when they'd shaken hands. Ew.

The guy had looked awkward, arms hanging by his sides, his posture rigid. It reminded her of one of her fellow models with Asperger's. Hyper-focused on one thing or person at a time.

Sam put him out of her mind so she could wallow in self-pity.

Hiding in plain sight was more difficult than she imagined. Without a rigid schedule, Sam found herself binge-watching cooking shows and eating all the foods she'd been denied for the past eight years. Premade enchiladas, bagels with cream cheese, frozen waffles.

All these items made it into her Instacart order, delivered same day or the next. Pure bliss.

The doorbell rang, a discordant sound in the echoing stillness of the house. Sam tiptoed toward the door and pressed her eye to the peephole.

"Lauren," she exclaimed, unlocking the door and pulling it open.

Her sister carried a pink bakery box. "I brought muffins," Lauren said, stepping into the house.

"When do you have time to bake?"

"Sorry to disappoint you, but Kennedy made these." She set the box on the kitchen island and looked around. "Nice digs. Is your dishwasher broken?" Lauren pointed to the dirty dishes and flatware piled in the sink and on the counter.

Sam shrugged. "I have no idea."

Lauren narrowed her eyes. "You're a slob."

"Am not."

Lauren tilted her head toward the sink. "Are too."

"I'm gonna tell Mom."

Lauren burst out laughing. Sam joined her.

"I'm so glad you came, Sis. I needed this."

"Why don't you make some coffee while I throw these dishes in the dishwasher." Lauren shot her a cocky look. "You *do* know how to make coffee, right?"

"Now *that* I can do." Sam bustled around, dumping coffee beans into the Breville Barista Express machine. Soon the fragrance of fresh coffee filled the kitchen.

"What I couldn't do in a kitchen like this," Lauren

said.

Sam took in the kitchen, seeing it from Lauren's eyes. Dark marble covered the island with lighter marble on the surrounding countertops. The modern cabinets were medium gray with brushed metal pulls. The sub-zero refrigerator sat next to the Bosch dishwasher.

Sam snickered. "First of all, you have a fabulous kitchen in your soon-to-be home on Lake Keuka. Second, I don't cook. You know that." She waved around at the modern appliances. "I wouldn't know what to do in here. Now, enough talk. I want a muffin."

When the coffees were done, Sam and Lauren headed into the combination dining and living room. Lauren walked to the French doors and gazed out at the lake.

"Beautiful view, isn't it?" Sam said.

"Yes, it is. I wish you'd have rented a place closer to me and Paul."

"Yeah. Wasn't my choice, though."

Sam set the mugs on the dining table and opened the box. "I'm gonna have two of these bad boys," she said, reaching for a muffin.

Lauren moved to the table and sat. "Thanks for the coffee."

Sam took a huge bite of muffin and spoke around it. "You've lost weight," she said, eyeing her sister from the chest up.

"And you've gained."

Sam frowned. "Don't tell me you're channeling Mom."

"Gosh, no. I'd never do that. I've dealt with enough body-shaming from her to last me six lifetimes. What I meant was, you look great."

"Huh. I'm feeling a bit, I don't know, puffy." Sam took another bite. "I'm eating my frustration over being trapped here."

Lauren sent her a sympathetic look. "I'm sorry. That's gotta be tough."

"I keep hearing Mom harp on me about my weight."

Lauren dropped her muffin on the table where it rolled onto the floor. "You never told me Mom body-shamed you too."

Sam felt the familiar slow churn of her stomach remembering the way Mom constantly reminded her not to gain weight.

Sam took a sip of her espresso and said, "It wasn't until I got out on my own that she stopped nagging me. She was terrified I'd gain a pound and lose a modeling contract. It took me months of therapy to overcome my tendency toward anorexia."

Lauren leaned over to pick up the muffin from the floor. "I had no idea," she whispered. "I thought I was the only one she tormented."

"Nope. Since I was fourteen and got my first job. She monitored every calorie, every ounce of food." Sam huffed a humorless laugh. "Did you know I had my first Oreo yesterday?"

"How was it?"

"A-*mazing*. Did you know you can pop them apart and lick the frosting off the middle?"

"It's a well-known fact that's the only way to eat an Oreo."

"What else have I missed?"

Lauren snorted. "I could write a book."

"In the meantime, I guess I'll have to continue experimenting on my own."

Both women turned to look when they heard a quick rap on the French doors. Mandy stood with her hand raised to knock again.

"Who's that?" Lauren asked.

Sam scraped her chair back. "That's the girl who lives next door. Come on, I'll introduce you. She's a sweet kid."

Lauren quirked an eyebrow. "Is her dad single?"

"I have no idea and I don't care."

"Just wondering," Lauren said with a grin.

Logan's pronouncement as he and Mandy sat down to lunch didn't have the response he expected.

"I signed you up for summer lacrosse at the community center. You start tomorrow."

"What?" Mandy's mouth dropped open and closed with a snap. "No. You can't make me."

"You're not going to sit around here all summer playing video games and texting your friends about how bored you are."

"Bruh, are you trying to kill me right now?"

Logan raised his eyebrows. "Don't 'bruh' me. I'm your father."

Mandy mumbled something that might have been an apology.

"I told Sam I'd hang out with her today," Mandy said.

"You'll be back in plenty of time to hang out. Besides, I want you to make some friends your own age." Not some modeling assistant next door.

Mandy grabbed her phone and typed furiously with her thumbs.

"Who are you texting?"

"My friends. Telling them I have the meanest dad in the universe."

Logan resisted the urge to roll *his* eyes. Too bad there wasn't a manual on how to raise a teenage daughter as a single dad when you have a ton of money at your disposal.

"I'll tell you what. Try it for a week, and it you hate it, you can quit. Deal?"

Mandy eyed him suspiciously. "For reals?"

"For reals." Logan stuck out his hand to make it formal.

Mandy's deep sigh made Logan want to smile. But he forced his mouth to remain neutral. His daughter's hand barely fit in his. She'd probably be tall like her mom. And beautiful, once she grew into her face.

Braces encased her teeth like little barbed wire fences and a bit of baby chubbiness still filled her cheeks.

Based on his research, it was possible Mandy could grow to as much as six feet in height. He'd have to steer her away from modeling as a career. That was one of the arrows that destroyed his marriage.

"I'm going to my room." Mandy picked up her plate and carried it in one hand, phone in the other.

Logan watched her retreat up the stairs and heard the door slam.

"Carmen, I'll be outside if you need me." He grabbed his laptop and headed for the deck. Opening his laptop, he was soon immersed in his latest project.

Sometime later, his concentration was interrupted.

"Dad."

Logan looked up and focused on his daughter's frowning face.

"I've been calling your name for, like, an hour."

Logan rubbed a hand across his eyes. "Sorry. I was immersed."

"Obvs. I'm going next door to see Sam."

Why did her pronouncement bother him so much? Was Mandy so starved for female attention she'd latched on to some random person next door?

"I don't think so," Logan said.

Mandy stamped her foot. "She's expecting me, Dad. You always said I need to honor my commitments. Sam told me to come over today and hang out." Mandy stood, hands on hips, daring him to argue.

Logan glanced up at the deck of the rental and back down to his daughter. "Fine. Check with me in an hour."

Mandy didn't respond. He watched her long legs eat up the distance between his house and the rental. She took the rental's wood steps two at a time. Her natural grace reminded him of a ballet dancer. Maybe he should enroll her in dance lessons instead of lacrosse. Logan tucked that thought into a compartment to pull out and dissect later. Right now, he had more research to do on his latest project.

Facial recognition and border control security.

Chapter 5

Samantha's heart sped up when she heard footsteps on the deck stairs. A moment later, Mandy came into view. Good. It was only the girl and not her nerdy dad.

"Hey," Mandy said, dropping onto a deck chair. "Want to hang out? Did your sister leave?"

Sam let the magazine she'd been thumbing through drop to the deck. "Lauren left a while ago. What do you want to do?" How did one amuse a teenager?

"Wanna play a game?"

"Do you know how to play cribbage?" Sam chuckled at the confused look on the girl's face. "It's a combo of a card game and board game. Sort of."

Mandy shrugged. "I guess."

"Please curb your enthusiasm," Sam said, getting up from the lounger. "I'll be right back."

She found the cribbage board and a deck of cards in

her Foldie bag and returned to the deck. "Pull that little table over," she said.

Sam and Mandy sat across from each other while Sam shuffled and explained the rules. "There's two parts to this game. There's pegging and there's counting the points in your hand."

Mandy paid close attention to Sam's explanation. "Got it. Can we do, like, an open hand to start?"

"Of course," Sam replied, dealing six cards to each. She laid her hand on the table. Mandy did the same.

It only took the girl a couple of open deals before she picked up a rudimentary understanding of the game. Sam easily won.

"Again?" Sam asked.

"Let me text my dad and let him know you haven't sold me into slavery yet." This was said with an exaggerated eye roll.

"He's super protective, isn't he?" Sam observed. "How old are you?"

"Fourteen."

Sam remembered being escorted to photo shoots by her mom when she was Mandy's age. Mom hovered around the set with watchful eyes, wary of anyone who got too close. Except that one time. The memory still brought a cold chill up her spine.

"It's normal for a dad to be protective."

Mandy snorted. "He's anything but normal. My dad gets super-focused on stuff. Like crazy focused."

That would explain the intensity of the man's gaze.

"What does your dad do? For work, that is."

"I have no idea. Nothing, I think. I mean, he's like, always hunched over his laptop. But since he sold some invention he created, he hasn't had, like, a real job."

Sam digested this for a moment. "Did you get a response from your text?"

Mandy stared down at the phone in her hand. "Not yet. But that's okay. Once he concentrates on something, he loses connection with the real world."

Sam could relate in a way. When she was on set or on location, her goal was solely on the next pose. Hours would sometimes pass before they'd break, and Sam would realize she was not only starving but dead on her feet.

"Let's go swimming," Mandy said, stretching her arms above her head.

Sam grimaced. "No, I don't think so. I'm not much of a swimmer."

Mandy snapped her fingers. "I know. Let's talk my dad into taking us out on the sailboat." She stood and walked to the edge of the deck and leaned over the railing. "Dad!"

Sam's pulse sped up. *Low profile. Low profile.* She joined Mandy at the railing. "I don't think I can go."

Mandy whirled to face her. "But it's so much fun. You're not afraid of the water, are you?"

It wasn't fear of the water that had her hands shaking. It was being exposed out on lake. What if . . .

"I'll be right back," Mandy said, sprinting down the

steps and over to where her dad sat on the deck in the shade.

The wind pushed their voices away, but from their body language, Mandy was doing her best to convince her dad. The four-person sailboat sat bobbing in the water on one side of the pier. What would it feel like to have the wind blow her hair back? Real wind, not from a wind machine on location. Freedom. That's what it would feel like.

Mandy turned and gave two thumbs up accompanied by a huge grin. She cupped her hands around her mouth and shouted, "I'm gonna put my suit on. Meet us down there." She pointed to the boat.

Sam sucked in a breath. "Okay," she yelled back. She'd put her swimsuit on, but the cut off sweat pants and baggy t-shirt would go over it. She wasn't giving Mandy's dad a glimpse of her swimsuit clad body.

She took a moment to laugh at herself. She had no problem wearing a backless dress or low-cut top in front of the camera. But with some man she'd just met? Nope.

Sam strode through the house, dropping articles of clothing on the floor as she made her way to the bedroom.

Why had he let Mandy wear him down? Being this close to a strange woman made his mouth dry and his palms sweat. Logan pushed his glasses up his nose and pulled the bill of his cap lower. He'd barely glanced at her when she climbed into *Small Fry*, his four-person daysailer. Her large sunglasses obscured most of her face, as did the straw sunhat.

Mandy bounced up and down in excitement. He'd forgotten to remind her about wearing a life jacket and now they were a hundred yards out on the lake, the life jackets still on the deck. He shuddered to think what would happen if they capsized.

This time of year, the water temperature may have reached a safe seventy degrees. Maybe. But swimming out here was fraught with danger. He'd never get over it if something happened to his daughter.

"Dad, when we get out in the middle, can we go swimming?"

"No."

His back was to her, but Logan imagined the face she'd make as she wound up to argue.

"I probably won't swim," Sam said.

Logan silently thanked her. "The water's too cold yet, Mandy."

He turned to see her plunge her hand into the lake.

"It's not." Her look challenged him to argue.

Rather than be sucked into an argument he may or may not win, he addressed Sam for the first time. Her knuckles were white as she gripped the side of the boat.

"Are you nervous?" Logan asked.

"A little. I've actually never been on a boat this small."

"This is a fourteen-foot daysailer. It's made specifically for up to four passengers. As the name implies, they are intended for day use. Mine is equipped with a small outboard motor, as you may have noticed."

Mandy rolled her eyes. "Thank you, Mr. Google."

Logan pressed his lips together.

Sam smiled. "I like the name you've given her. *Small Fry*."

"It came with the boat." Logan didn't intend to sound terse. "Mandy, help me unfurl the sails."

Mandy jumped up, and the boat rocked as she expertly unhooked the sails from the mast. Soon the wind grabbed the fabric, and the boat skimmed over the waves.

He glanced at Sam. Her grip had loosened, and she seemed slightly more relaxed. She tilted her head back and Logan saw the sleek line of her neck. He moved to the back of the boat and sat, taking the seat Mandy vacated.

"Mandy, you're in charge," he said. She nodded her agreement and grinned.

"You've never been sailing before?" Logan asked.

"I didn't say that," Sam replied. "I said I'd never been on a boat this small."

When she didn't elaborate, he said, "But you've been sailing."

Sam's chest expanded under her T-shirt as she inhaled. "I've been on location on an Oceano ship."

Logan whistled. "That's a huge vessel. Over a

hundred twenty feet in length."

Sam clapped a hand on her hat to keep it from blowing off as their speed increased. Logan admired her profile. His face warmed as she turned and caught him staring. The wind blew her hair back and he could see her flawless porcelain skin. Too bad those huge sunglasses hid her eyes. Why would someone so pretty hide under ugly sunglasses and bulky clothing?

Who did she remind him of? His brain began a series of facial shots, much like paging through a mug shot binder. There was something about her that niggled at the edge of his brain.

Logan tamped down the attraction he felt as he gazed at her profile. She was a temporary renter of his home next door. She'd be gone in a couple of months, and he'd be alone again. Which was where he felt the most comfortable. His own space.

The attraction he'd felt for his ex, Mandy's mom, was similar. What she'd seen in him was still a mystery. They'd gotten married in a flurry, and Viv had gotten pregnant almost immediately. She'd seen him as an escape from a violent living situation, and he'd seen her as someone to help him feel normal.

Their marriage was anything but normal. Vivian had blossomed late into a willowy beauty. A modeling agency picked her out of a crowd. She'd had a successful career as a Victoria's secret model, to Mandy's extreme embarrassment.

After their divorce, Vivian took Mandy to

California and only recently returned to New York. Logan was left alone, as he preferred.

But now Viv had decided it was time for Logan to be a full-time dad so she could live in Italy with her new husband.

Sam turned and caught Logan staring. He couldn't see her eyes. Was she amused that he couldn't keep his eyes off her? That someone as dull as he would find her attractive? She was probably laughing at him behind those shades. Like every other woman.

Logan sucked in his stomach and pulled his T-shirt down. Like it would help.

Chapter 6

Sam stood under the scalding hot shower, washing the sweat and sunscreen down the drain. "That was fun," she said aloud. Gliding over the wake from ski boats had made the little sailboat rock and bounce. Once she realized they wouldn't capsize, Sam relaxed and enjoyed the sun and fresh air. What a difference from the huge sailboat she'd posed on for a summer *Vogue* photo layout. There hadn't been time to relax then. After the shoot, they'd returned to shore, and Sam had taxied to her apartment to crash. Two hours of hair and makeup plus eight hours of looking glamorous took its toll. Such was her life.

She loved it. Most of the time.

She closed her eyes against the pulsing spray and silently cursed her stalker.

Logan had been nice to give into Mandy's insistence that Sam be invited. She'd caught him staring at her more than once. She was used to men staring, but his gaze was different. Almost like he was memorizing her features.

Logan was polar opposite of the men Sam knew. Skinny male models, shallow and narcissistic. Not all of them, but enough to be cautious if anyone happened to ask her out. Her standard excuse. 'I don't date anyone in the industry,' was usually taken without rancor. Her publicist kept her social calendar filled with opportunities to be seen with people who mattered.

But Logan. Something about him gave her pause. He was sweet in a nerdy sort of way. Generic black framed glasses and longish hair. Slight paunch around his middle. Swim trunks and a T-shirt he probably bought at Walmart. No designer label to be seen.

Mandy on the other hand, must have someone to help her shop. Her mom, maybe. Mandy's clothes screamed designer. Why the dichotomy?

Sam turned off the shower and tried to picture the type of man she wanted to spend her life with. Definitely someone who wouldn't be jealous of her career. Nor try to compete. She'd felt a tiny spark when Logan had helped her out of his little boat. His hand was dry and warm, not the icky damp of their first meeting.

Sam laughed at herself for thinking there'd been a spark.

"You are getting crazy, girlfriend. You're only here for a short time until your stalker is caught."

Saying the words out loud didn't sit well. The few days she'd been staying here had been relaxing.

Sleeping in, eating what she wanted, and responsible for nothing. Except for the loneliness, this would be a great vacation.

Dressed in a loose pair of pajama bottoms and an oversized T-shirt, Sam sunk onto the cushy sofa and flipped on the big screen television in the living room. Her phone rang and she pulled it toward her.

"Kayleigh, what's up girlfriend? I haven't talked to you in ages."

"Hey, bestie," Kayleigh responded. "I'm calling to check in. Where are you? On some exotic location no doubt."

Sam groaned. "Not even. I'm actually in a rental house in Lake Skaneateles." Sam let her gaze travel around the room. Not exotic, but definitely comfortable.

"Are you doing a photo shoot on the lake?"

Sam quickly brought her best friend up to date on the situation with the stalker and her reasons for flying under the radar.

"That's awful! I'll bet you're terrified."

"You could say that," Sam agreed. "But talk to me about you. How's Nashville?"

It was Kayleigh's turn to groan. "Nashville is a lot like New York City. The sidewalks are full of tourists. Everybody is hoping to see Garth Brooks or Carrie Underwood. The traffic is unbelievable. But there's good music everywhere."

"Which is why you're there. What's happening with your music career."

"Meh. Not much. I got a job as a waitress in a bar, like every other aspiring singer songwriter. The manager keeps telling me I'll get my chance to perform. But so far, nada. Zip."

"I'm sorry. Hang in there, girl. You've got talent."

Kayleigh laughed. "There's talent and then there's talent. I have small-town, rural New York talent. What I need is Big City talent."

"Your time will come. What's new on the dating scene? Seeing anyone?"

"Nope. The guys here are all macho cowboys looking to be the next Toby Keith." Kayleigh breathed a dramatic sigh. "I can't even. How about you? Any hot guys in swim trunks on Lake Skaneateles?"

Sam's mind immediately thought of Logan. 'Hot' wasn't a word she'd use to describe him. Logan definitely had 'dad bod.' When he'd stripped off his shirt to jump into the lake with Mandy, she'd glimpsed his slight paunch and arms that could use a gym workout. He'd removed the thick black-framed glasses to reveal his one redeeming feature. Brilliant green eyes.

"You're taking a long time to answer, girlfriend," Kayleigh said. "What's the tea?"

"I met this girl who lives next door."

"You're not into girls now, are you?" Kayleigh teased.

"She's fourteen, Kay. Anyway, she and her dad took me out on their sailboat today. It was fun."

"Hm. Single dad of a teenage daughter. Sounds interesting."

"He's kinda cute in a nerdy sort of way."

"So, totally opposite of the guys you normally go out with."

"Yup. Not super skinny and narcissistic. And not a movie star. Besides, the only reason I go out with those guys is because it makes for good press."

"For you or for them?" Count on Kayleigh to get to the heart of the matter.

"Both." Sam's publicist found plenty of opportunities for Sam to be arm candy for some up-and-coming movie star or pop singer. It kept their names in the limelight. Most of the time, Sam didn't mind. She and the guy knew it was all for the paparazzi. A problem occurred only if the guy became handsy or thought that a night on his arm meant she'd hop into the sack with him when the event was over.

"Sucks to be you," Kayleigh said with a laugh.

"Yeah, well at the moment it truly does suck. Now that I'm hiding, it's scary."

"Sweetie, I'm sorry. I know it must be awful. Oh, I gotta go. My break is over, and my manager is sending me death looks."

"Okay, bestie. Love you."

"Love you too. Send me a pic of your new identity."

Sam disconnected. Between her sister, Lauren, and her bestie, she was lucky. A lot of her model friends had only superficial relationships. It was tough to keep friends when you traveled all the time and had a crazy schedule.

"Everyone thinks being a model is glamorous," she said aloud. They didn't see the darker side of the business. Like being stalked by someone.

Logan pulled his laptop closer and focused on the screen as his fingers tapped his next-door neighbor's name into the search engine. Vera Samuels.

Nothing.

Logan tried a different search engine. This time the search brought up the obituary for a Black woman and another for an English tutor who didn't resemble his next door neighbor in the least.

Who was she? Wasn't every twenty-something on social media? Logan focused his attention to the rental agreement. Although he'd memorized it months ago when he'd purchased the home next door, he reread it searching for a clue as to why a modeling agency would put someone up in the rental who obviously wasn't a model.

Logan glanced into the living room and was relieved to see Mandy hadn't come out of the bathroom yet. He placed a call to the agency.

"Top Notch Talent. How may I direct your call?" The receptionist's voice was chirpy and crisp.

"This is Logan Walters. Please direct me to the person responsible for renting a house on Skaneateles

Lake."

Canned music blasted through the phone while Logan waited.

"This is Marshall Goodman. How may I help you?"

"I'm trying to get some information about the house your agency rented on Lake Skaneateles here in New York."

"And you are?" The man sounded snooty. Logan pictured him as some skinny jeans-wearing man bun guy.

"I'm Logan Walters, and the rental belongs to me."

"One moment."

Logan clamped his teeth together as he was placed on hold again.

Five minutes later, the man came back on the phone. "I apologize for the delay. I am not able to give you information at this time."

"But—"

"Is there a problem with the renter? A complaint you'd like to register?"

"No, it's not—"

"If you have an issue with the person or persons renting the house, I suggest you put the complaint in writing. You can reach us through the contact form on our website. www.TopNotchTalent(dot)com."

Before Logan could react, the call was disconnected. What the what?

He tapped out an email to his virtual assistant.

Can you get some more information on the person

renting next door?

Logan hesitated with his fingers hovering over the keyboard. What else should he add? How to explain to his VA that once he focused on some minute detail, he was like a drug-sniffing dog. He wouldn't be satisfied until he figured out who Vera Samuels was.

Not long after he completed the email, Mandy pulled out a chair and sat with him at the table.

"Whatcha doin'?" she asked.

Logan snapped the lid of his Mac down. "Research."

Mandy yawned. "That was fun today. We should do it again tomorrow."

"Tomorrow you have lacrosse at one."

Mandy groaned. "Do I have to?"

"We have a deal. One week. Remember?"

Mandy slumped down. "Okay. But after that I'm going to see Sam. She's teaching me to play cribbage."

After Mandy shuffled to her bedroom, Logan searched online for the rules to cribbage.

"Doesn't look too difficult," he said. He committed the rules to memory and made a plan to learn more about Sam over a friendly game of cribbage.

Chapter 7

"I'm officially bored out of my skull," Sam said. She stood at the kitchen window shoveling spoonsful of Honey Nut Cheerios into her mouth. A courier in a white van pulled up in front of the house. A young woman jumped out with a parcel and approached the door.

Sam hurried to intercept the woman.

"Hi," she said, holding her hand out for the package.

"Package for Samantha Jensen."

"That's me."

"I need to scan it real quick." The courier held out a bulky device and moved it over the address label.

"How's your day going?" Sam asked. Anything to keep a conversation going.

The woman glanced up and back down to her scanner. "Fine." She stepped back and turned toward the waiting van. "Have a nice day."

Sam exhaled. Darn. But at least she had the

package. The return address was Top Notch Talent. Must be something from Skyler. Speaking of which, her manager had never called or texted. That was troubling.

Sam closed the front door and locked it. She returned to the kitchen and went on a hunt for a pair of scissors. Several drawers later, she found them. A stack of glossy fashion magazines poured out of the package onto the counter.

"Ooh, goodie. Something to look at."

Sam carried the bundle to the dining room table and fanned them out. Which one to peruse first? She pulled *Elle* toward her and flipped through the pages. Her publicist had marked several places with skinny sticky notes.

This was the part Sam hated. She opened to her fashion spread to the page marked and read the comments her publicist had written in black ink.

The first one was scrawled on a photo of her in a Dior gown. 'Next time, turn more to the side so we can see the straps crisscrossing the back.'

Each photo had critiques. Sam stuck out her tongue. Her very picky publicist, Manny, never had a good word.

Sam closed the magazine and pulled *Cosmo* toward her. She hated having her picture in this rag but Skyler and Manny agreed it raised her image.

More like dragged it down.

Sam flipped through the pages to find photos of her with Dawson Knox. He was described as the next Harry

Stiles.

'Super model Samantha Jensen was seen being escorted to the New York Children's Hospital fundraising gala by Dawson Knox. Knox sported a slate gray Brioni, while Jensen wore a dress by a new designer, Alexandra.'

The article went on to describe their clothes down to the tiniest detail.

"Wonder why they didn't mention our underwear," Sam said with a chuckle.

Her phone rang and Lauren's picture filled the screen.

"What's up, Sis?" Sam asked.

"Have you seen the latest *People* magazine?"

Sam glanced over the spread on the table. "Nope. I just got a bunch of mags, but no *People*. Why?"

"There's a blurb on you. Want me to read it?"

"Sure." Seeing her picture in *People* didn't thrill her like it did when she started her career. She was usually caught with her mouth open or in an awkward position.

"It says, 'Rumors are swirling about supermodel Samantha Jensen. She's disappeared off the social scene and has dropped out of sight. Some speculate she's in rehab while others claim they've seen her in Las Vegas. Is a quickie marriage to pop star Dawson Knox in Ms. Jensen's future?'"

Sam closed her eyes and prayed for patience. "Good grief."

"Want me to send it to you? I can take a

screenshot."

"Don't bother. I'm used to it. But the part about rehab . . ." Sam stood and walked to the French doors. She'd opened the side windows, and a cool breeze brought fresh air into the house. "I didn't know you read *People* magazine."

Lauren laughed. "I don't. Kennedy saw it."

"Wait, what? Your purple-haired tattooed former employee reads *People*?"

"She's hardly a fan. She took Molly to the groomer and paged through it while she waited."

Sam smiled, remembering how Lauren had debated for days before hiring Kennedy. Lauren had been worried the woman would scare off the little old ladies who came in for their morning muffin and coffee. Now that Lauren had gifted the bakery to her, Kennedy had thrived in her new position as business owner.

All because Sam's big sister fell in love with a billionaire. Sam smiled to herself. The only available man in her orbit was a nerdy divorced guy with a teenage daughter.

Lauren's voice interrupted Sam's mental meanderings. "I gotta run. Paul is whisking me off to Florida to say hi to Mom and Dad."

"Ugh. Sucks to be you."

"Agreed. But even Mom is softening. Wait till she finds out he's a Republican."

Sam and Lauren shared a laugh before they disconnected.

Sam grabbed *Vogue* and sauntered out to the deck. Bracing herself for the next round of criticism from Manny, she sank down on the padded lounger and was soon engrossed in the glossy pages.

Logan's concentration was interrupted by Mandy tapping him on the shoulder.

"Earth to Dad."

Logan blinked, closed his laptop, and turned to face his daughter. "Huh?"

She rolled her eyes. "If you want me to go to lacrosse, we better go."

"Oh, right. Lacrosse. Sure." Concentration broken, Logan stood and stretched. "Let me grab my keys and wallet and we'll go."

Logan asked himself how in the world he would be able to parent Mandy and work on his latest project. His tendency to dive into research and coding made him oblivious to food, time, and bodily functions.

Darn you, Vivian. Once his ex decided to flit off to Italy with her new husband, she'd dropped their daughter off with hardly a backward glance. The few weeks he got to spend with Mandy did not prepare him for being a full-time dad.

"Give me your phone," Mandy demanded when they'd climbed into his Aston Martin.

"Why?"

"I'm going to set an alarm for when it's time to

come get me." Mandy sent him a knowing look.

Logan couldn't help but smile. "Good idea." Maybe this single parent thing could work. Maybe.

After dropping Mandy at the community center and getting her settled, Logan returned home and walked out to the deck. Resting his hands on the rail, he leaned out and gulped in the fresh air blowing over the lake. The breeze carried hints of chicken roasting on a barbecue and faint wisps of suntan lotion. Retrieving a pair of binoculars from a waterproof storage container, he focused on the homes across the expanse of crystal blue water.

Rumor had it the Clintons and Obamas had homes on this lake. Logan swept the binoculars from side to side, hoping to get a glimpse of someone famous. The world of the rich and famous still fascinated him, even though he'd joined the rich part of their ranks after the sale of his facial-recognition software. But aside of the purchase of this home and the one next door, and his imported vehicle, Logan preferred to keep a low profile.

His numerous charitable donations were made through a generic trust. He had no wish to be part of the billionaire social scene. But it might be cool to catch a glimpse of a famous politician.

A chirp from his phone showed movement at the front door. Carmen entered the house carrying the day's mail. Logan met her at the sliding door.

"Here's your mail, Mr. Logan."

A few pieces of junk mail sat atop this week's

People magazine. Logan took the stack from her without comment. For all Carmen knew, the magazine was for Mandy. So what if he had an obsession over movie stars.

Footsteps on the wood deck next door caught his attention. His neighbor, Sam, raised a hand and waved when she saw him looking. Before he could second-guess himself, Logan stepped off his deck and crossed the berm to his rental. He bounded up the steps to where Sam sat at the patio table, thumbing through a glossy fashion magazine.

"Hi, neighbor," she greeted him. A wood cribbage board sat on the table.

"Mandy said you are teaching her to play," Logan said, pointing at the board.

Sam smiled. "Oh, yes. She's a fast learner. It took me days to learn, but she's already picking it up. Do you play?"

"I've read the rules."

"But do you play?" Sam's question hung in the air.

"I could try."

"Sit. Let's see how you do, Mr. I Read The Rules."

Logan's face grew warm. He used his index finger to push his glasses up.

Sam shuffled the deck with expert moves. Logan admired the way her long fingers manipulated the cards, making a sharp whooshing sound.

"Since you're read the rules, I'll deal and we'll see how you do." Sam's eyes narrowed as she smiled with a calculating look.

Logan's mouth went dry. Despite her colorful, weird haircut and ill-fitting clothes, his neighbor was an attractive woman. Or was he so desperate for companionship that she looked good? Pretty women never gave him a second glance. Logan was self-aware enough to know he was not the type of man to be a chick magnet. Until they found out he was wealthy. His self-imposed isolation kept him from predators of the female variety. But his current lifestyle wasn't healthy for his daughter.

He'd think about that later. Right now, he needed to focus on the game of Cribbage.

Chapter 8

While they played, Sam peppered Logan with questions. Logan's short answers confirmed his concentration on the game.

"How long have you lived here on the lake?"

"I was born near here."

"In Lake Skaneateles?"

"Nearby."

"How long have you lived in this house?"

"Two years and three months."

"Do you leave during the winter?"

"Yes."

Sam huffed in frustration. She wanted a real conversation with a human being. Instead, she got robot-man. Mandy had said her dad became ultra-focused on things. He must be concentrating on actually playing the game of Cribbage rather than reading about it. She stopped talking until she won the first game.

"Nice try, Mr. Rules," she said, scooping up the cards. "Another?"

Logan glanced at his phone. "I don't have time. I have to leave soon to pick Mandy up from lacrosse."

"She didn't seem super excited about it."

"No, she didn't." Logan grimaced. "I don't want her to be bored all summer."

"Makes sense."

Logan's eyes traveled over her assortment of magazines. Sam bit her lip, wondering if she should explain.

"No *People* magazine?" Logan said with the ghost of a smile.

"Ahh, no." Sam waved a hand over the magazines "I have to keep up with what's trending in the industry." Had she mentioned she was a pretend model assistant?

"I see." Logan scraped back his chair and stood. "I better go. Mandy will kill me if I'm late."

"Wait. I just remembered you had some mail that was delivered here by mistake." Sam dashed into the house and retrieved the postcard addressed to Logan Walters.

She'd read the missive because she was nosy. Waving the postcard at him, she said, "This looks fun. You gonna go?"

Sam waited while Logan read the information about forming a committee to plan the fifteen-year Lake Skaneateles class reunion.

"No." Logan folded the card in half and shoved it into his back pocket.

"Why not? They could use your help, and it doesn't look like you're that busy." Why had she mentioned she'd spied on him? She waved a dismissive hand. "You could get Mandy to help, too. That would keep her occupied."

"I'll think about it."

Sheesh. This man was impossible.

"Promise?" Sam asked pressing the issue.

"Promise what?"

"To think about it."

Logan's eyes fixed on something over her right shoulder. "Fine."

Sam pinched her lips together and shook her head. She'd mention it to Mandy herself the next time the girl came over.

"Thanks for the game," Sam said.

"I'll try harder next time," Logan said, turning to leave. He mumbled something under his breath that Sam didn't catch.

Logan paused at the top of the steps. "Are you on social media?"

"No. Why?" That came out of nowhere. As her real self, she was on social media. Her publicist took care of posting photos and updates. But as Vera Samuels, there wasn't anything to connect her to Samantha Jensen.

"No reason."

Sam watched him disappear down the steps. That was weird. She returned to the stack of magazines and paged through her spread for Marc Jacobs. Hair and makeup had spent a ridiculous amount of time on her appearance despite the focus on the handbags. Manny had only one comment scrawled across the bottom of the spread. 'Looking good.'

Sam felt a flush of pleasure. She could count on one hand Manny's positive comments.

"It's a win!" Sam declared aloud. She raised both arms in a gesture of triumph.

Letting her arms fall, Sam squinted into the sunlight glinting off Lake Skaneateles. A feeling of helplessness overwhelmed her. Her only form of human contact was playing a stupid card game with a teenager and her father. Trapped by her own quasi-celebrity. A face recognized in the fashion and entertainment industry.

"Look at me now." Sam ran a hand down the pink cotton pants. They were supposed to be capris, but they looked like someone had chopped off a pair of pants and hemmed them. The flowered blouse wasn't much better. She looked like she'd raided Granny's closet.

Without makeup, her eyebrows and eyelashes faded into invisibility. Even her lips looked pale.

Sam jumped up from the deck chair and strode into the house. In the bathroom, she dumped out her cosmetic bag onto the counter.

The La Prairie foundation exactly matched her skin tone. After spreading it over her face, Sam added a bit of blush. Then she went to work on her eyebrows, coloring them with a brown pencil. Once they were visible, she added a hint of mascara.

Soft pink lipstick went on last.

There was nothing she could do with her hair, but staring at her reflection in the bathroom mirror brought a sense of satisfaction. This was who she was. Beautiful, photogenic, hard-working Sumatran Jensen. Supermodel.

Tears filled her eyes at the unfairness of her current situation. How dare some random guy decide to make her life miserable? It was too much like the time when she was sixteen.

That one photographer who lingered, waiting for the moment her mom disappeared from view. Sam shivered as the memory flooded back, the unsettling sensation of his hands pressing against her skin, his hot breath against her neck. He had whispered vile, revolting things that made her stomach churn. The sense of entrapment, suffocating and palpable, was just as vivid now as it had been then.

Sam stumbled to the toilet and retched until her stomach was empty. After, she washed her face, letting the makeup swirl down the drain.

Mandy slid into the Aston Martin smelling of fresh cut grass and teenage angst.

"How was it?" Logan asked, shifting into drive.

Mandy shrugged. "Okay, I guess." She pulled her phone out and thumbed the screen.

"I brought you a bottle of water." Logan indicated

the bottle now sweating in the cup holder.

Mandy took it without comment, downing half in a few gulps.

"You're welcome." That elicited a side glance. Still no comment.

Logan let out a sigh. These teen years were going to be his biggest challenge. Gone were the days when Mandy came to see him excited about outings to the zoo, the aquarium, or to the park. What did one do with a recalcitrant teen?

His thoughts turned to the reunion postcard now stabbing him in his back pocket. He'd promised Sam he'd think about getting involved. The thought of interacting with his former high school classmates increased his pulse and made his stomach churn.

High school did not bring on his fondest memories. Awkward, pimple-faced, with thick glasses, all made him a target for bullying. Not to mention his Goodwill clothes. How his dad managed to provide him a place to live in the upscale community of the lake was beyond him. Dad's job with Glider Oil paid well, but Dad had a problem with gambling. After Mom left, his dad made no pretense in trying to hide his addiction.

Logan pulled up to the house. Mandy hopped out before the car barely rolled to a stop.

"I'm gonna take a shower and go next door. Sam promised me another lesson in cribbage."

She disappeared into the house. Logan sat in the car, listening to the tick-tick-tick of the engine as it cooled.

An hour later, Logan heard laughter coming from the deck next door. An unfamiliar emotion pushed on his chest. Jealousy. He was jealous of Sam enjoying time with his daughter. He was half-tempted to go over and tell Mandy it was time to come home.

He discarded that idea. She'd either argue with him or return home, sulky and angry. Logan picked up the *People* magazine and flipped through the pages to distract him.

The pages fell open to the gossip page.

"Rumors are swirling about supermodel Samantha Jensen. She's disappeared off the social scene and has dropped out of sight. Some speculate she's in rehab while others claim they've seen her in Las Vegas. Is a quickie marriage to pop star Dawson Knox in Ms. Jensen's future?"

Maybe Sam would have the inside scoop on the supermodel, since she was in the industry. Logan rolled the magazine up into one hand and headed next door. He found Mandy and Sam concentrating on the cards in their hands.

"Hey, Dad. What's up?" Finally, his daughter was talking to him again.

Logan made himself comfortable on the chair next to his daughter at the patio table. "Looks intense." Sam and Mandy's colored pegs were a few holes from the end. "Who's winning?"

Mandy shot him a triumphant grin. "I am."

Logan studied Sam to see if she might be letting his daughter win.

"But I get to count first," Sam said.

"Let's see if you have enough points to peg out." Mandy laid a card down as they progressed through the pegging part of the game.

Logan couldn't help being impressed his daughter was holding her own against an experienced player. But Sam had the points needed to win.

Sam raised her arms in victory. "I won!"

Mandy tossed her remaining cards on the table. "I was so close."

Sam scooped up the cards and straightened them into a neat stack. "Next time." She glanced at him. "Want to play?"

"Uh, no." He laid the *People* magazine on the table. Sam stiffened and her face lost all color.

Chapter 9

Sam stared at the magazine like it was a rattler about to strike. Her hands shook as she shoved the playing cards back into the box.

Logan's voice came through white noise clouding her ears.

"I wanted to ask you about something in *People*," he said.

No, no, no. Her cover couldn't have been blown already. Sam forced her breathing to return to normal.

"I can't believe you still read *People*, Dad," Mandy said, bumping him with her shoulder. Logan didn't answer. He flipped through the glossy pages of the magazine.

Logan located the sidebar and swiveled the magazine around to face her. "Do you know this person?" he asked, tapping a finger on the words.

Sam gulped. Time to deflect. "Why would a grown man read a rag like *People*?" She forced herself to smile and waggled her eyebrows.

Mandy laughed. "Exactly my question. Hm, Dad?"

A slight flush rose to Logan's cheeks. He raised his head to make eye contact. Sam was again taken aback by the emerald color of his eyes. If he were to ditch the black framed glasses for contacts and get a professional haircut, he would almost be good-looking. Almost.

Logan shifted his posture. "I'm interested in a lot of things."

"But *People* magazine, Dad? That's so basic."

Logan pointed toward Sam's stack of fashion magazines. "It's no different than those. Keeping up with current events is important."

Sam closed the magazine. "I may have met her at some event or other." She shifted under Logan's gaze.

"Has anyone ever told you you look a lot like Samantha Jensen?"

Sam's pulse spiked. "I get that a lot." Her voice came out higher than normal.

Mandy sent Sam an apologetic look. "You'll have to forgive my dad. He created this facial recognition thing and sold it for, like, a billion dollars. He's always staring at people's faces."

Sam huffed out a humorless laugh. Of all the rentals in New York State, her agency had chosen the one in a million home next to some guy who read faces.

Time to change the subject. "Did you talk to Mandy about helping with your class reunion committee?"

"Uh, no. I promised to think about it, not talk about

it."

"What committee?" Mandy asked, leaning toward her dad.

Sam smirked as Logan explained about the card he'd received.

"Your dad thought you might want to help too. Give you something to do."

"You'd be bored."

"Maybe. Maybe not," Mandy replied. "We should check it out. I can get all the dirty deets about what you were like in high school."

Logan cleared his throat. "I haven't made a decision yet."

"Oh, come on, Dad. I loved helping make the homecoming float at my school last year. It'll be fun. Please?"

Sam watched, amused, as Logan tried to curb Mandy's enthusiasm. Her amusement was quashed when Mandy added, "Sam can help too."

"I don't think that's a good idea," Sam said.

"That's correct, Mandy. Sam is here on vacation." The look Logan sent her wasn't quite convincing. Was he able to read her micro expressions? If so, he'd be able to read fear.

Low profile.

Mandy raised her hands. "You said you were bored, Sam."

"I don't think I said that." Had she? The truth was, she was bored. Lonely. Frustrated. Fearful.

Logan's steady gaze unnerved her. "Let's get home, Mandy." He stood and put out a hand for Mandy to take. She ignored it.

"Fine. But I still think it'll be fun." She huffed and shoved her chair back. "At least it'll be something to do instead of being held captive."

Sam pressed her lips together to keep from smiling at the teen's drama.

Later, after they'd gone home, Sam sat on the sofa picking at her nail polish. She was becoming attached to Mandy. The girl was a bundle of opposites. Her moods were like the dark clouds scuttling across the sky above the lake, followed by bursts of sunlight. Sam caught glimpses of the beauty Mandy would become once she grew into her body.

Logan was growing on her too. He couldn't be more different than the men Sam knew. Neither skinny, weight-conscious fellow models nor hunky movie star, Logan was almost a cliche. Nerdy software guy with a dad-bod. And he didn't have that calculating look of most men. The 'how can being with you benefit me' look. Or the 'I'm going to assume you're dumb because you're beautiful' look.

Just once, she'd like to have a normal relationship. A boyfriend. Was that too much to ask?

Logan was ready to agree to Mandy's suggestion, but Sam's reaction made him pause. He studied her posture, stiff and robotic, as she pulled the colored pegs from the cribbage board and stored them in the little compartment tucked into the back.

She'd been visibly shaken when he'd dropped the *People* magazine on the table. And now she looked ready to vomit at the suggestion she help with the class reunion committee.

"I'm sure Sam has plenty to do," Logan said, hoping to ease Sam's discomfort.

Mandy's head swiveled between him and Sam. "What is wrong with you people? Dad, you told me you didn't want my face buried in my phone all summer, but it's okay if you never leave your computer for more than, like, a minute." She turned to Sam. "What do you have to do?"

Sam smiled weakly. "I'm on vacation."

"Great. Then you have tons of time to help."

For a kid who had to be dragged to lacrosse, his daughter was now adamant about this class reunion project? Logan shook his head. He'd never understand the female species.

Logan stood. "Let's let Sam think about it, okay?" He rested his hand on Mandy's shoulder.

"Fine," Mandy said. "But you better say yes."

When they returned home, Logan opened his laptop and opened a new tab to search Top Notch Modeling. He located the portfolio for Samantha Jensen and scrolled through her photos. His next-door neighbor looked enough like the model to be her sister. The hair was different. Jensen's hair was long and blonde while Sam's was blue. He tried to picture Sam with makeup but couldn't quite. What he needed was a photo of his next-door neighbor.

Mandy's voice broke into his thoughts. "I want ice cream."

Logan snapped the laptop closed before Mandy could see the screen. "Huh?"

"Ice cream."

Logan squinted up at her. "What are you thinking?"

"I'm craving some mint chip. Remember that place you used to take me to?"

"Skan Ellis?"

"Yeah. Can we go? Please?"

Logan's heart warmed at his daughter's pleading face, reminding him of when she was a lot younger and going for ice cream was a huge treat. "Sure. Let me grab my keys."

Mandy's good mood lasted through the short car ride. She turned on the radio and sang to the oldies station songs.

"Remember when you let me get that triple-scoop cone?"

"And you threw up on the way home?" Logan reminded her.

Mandy laughed. "I thought you were going to puke too."

"I had to sell that car. I never got the smell out."

"Good times."

Logan grimaced when Mandy hung her arm out the window. He had visions of her arm getting hit by a passing light pole or tree. "Roll your window up, and I'll turn on the air conditioning."

"No way, Dad. It's perfect outside."

He would have insisted, but Mandy's mercurial mood might change in an instant if he did.

"I'd forgotten how good this is," Logan said as they sat outside eating their ice cream.

"We should come here for lunch sometime." Mandy licked a drip from the back of one hand. "We could bring Sam with us. She's bored."

"Why do you say that?"

Mandy shrugged. "Why else would she want to hang out with me?"

"Maybe she likes you."

"Maybe. Do you like her?"

Logan had no idea how to answer. Did he know Sam enough to know if he liked her? Why was she vacationing alone? Random questions pinged in his head until one landed and hit him like a dodgeball in the face. Top Notch Modeling rented his house where Sam was currently staying. The model, Samantha Jensen, worked for Top Notch Modeling. But when he pointed out the blurb in *People* magazine and asked if Sam knew her, she'd said, 'I might have run into her somewhere.'

The blurb also said Samantha Jensen had disappeared off the social scene.

Were Vera Samuels and Samantha Jensen the same person?

Chapter 10

The doorbell rang, rousing Sam from her comfy nest on the sofa. Peeking through the peephole, she found Lauren and her fiancé, Paul, standing on the front porch.

"Hi, guys. What brings you here?" Sam asked. She swung open the door to let them in.

"I brought some photos of possible bridesmaid's dresses, and I want to get your opinion."

"Anybody want coffee?" Sam asked, waving her half-empty mug.

"Sounds great," Lauren replied.

"Do you happen to have tea?" Paul asked.

Lauren's South African fiancé had spent enough time in England to prefer tea over coffee.

"I'm not sure," Sam said. "I can dig through the cupboards."

"No, don't bother."

Sam could see why Lauren had fallen for Paul. Tall, good-looking, and always polite. And his accent was adorable.

"Suit yourself," Sam said. She led them into the living room. "I'll get your coffee, Sis."

"This is a beautiful home," Paul commented.

"Isn't it?" Lauren replied. "I just wish Sam were closer to us."

"It's temporary, remember?" Sam called from the kitchen. She returned to the living room and handed Lauren a steaming cup of brew.

"How long do you expect to stay here?" Paul asked.

Sam let out a frustrated breath. "I have no idea. I need to call my manager. I'm hoping that since I haven't gotten any more creepy letters my stalker has lost interest."

Lauren shuddered. "I hate this."

Paul's phone chirped. Glancing at the screen, he said, "It's Marvin. I must take this."

Lauren flipped a hand toward him. "Why don't you take it outside?"

When Paul and stepped onto the back deck, Lauren plopped on the sofa next to Sam and opened up a pink portfolio. "Here's what I'm thinking."

They spent the next fifteen minutes flipping through pages of photos Lauren had downloaded.

"These look great, Lauren. I think I'm partial to the Mori Lee ones. What about you?"

"Sure. I want you to be comfortable."

"If I don't get back to work soon and, on a schedule, I'm going to need you to order me a plus-size." Sam patted her tummy. "All I do is eat and watch TV."

"I think you look great." Lauren reached over Sam's shoulder and pulled her close.

"Thanks. But I feel like a blimp." After years of watching every morsel of food, she'd used this situation to binge on everything she'd denied herself. Rice, pasta, cheese, and anything sweet. She was like an alcoholic in a liquor store.

"Let's talk more wedding stuff," Lauren said.

Sam let herself be pulled into Lauren's excitement. She'd never seen her sister so happy. After that other guy broke her heart, she'd found her happily ever after. Sam quickly quashed the bit of jealousy that flared. Lauren deserved to be happy. Paul treated her like the treasure she was.

Sam had been too busy with her career to want romance. But now that she was alone, she felt she'd missed out. It was difficult, if not impossible to have a relationship when her schedule could sometimes be erratic. If a shoot was held up because of weather or any one of a number of unforeseen circumstances, dates would have to be canceled. If her publicist thought she wasn't getting enough attention, he'd arrange a date with a movie star. How to explain to a man that it was all for show? Anyone not in the business didn't understand.

Sam wallowed in self-pity, even while joining Lauren in the discussion about flowers, music, and food for the reception.

Paul stepped back into the house.

"Everything okay?" Lauren asked.

Paul strode over and planted a kiss on Lauren's forehead. "Perfect," he said, gazing into her eyes.

The jealousy Sam thought she'd doused flared into a blazing inferno. She'd never have a man look at her like that. Even her temporary next-door-neighbor watched her like he was trying to figure her out. His whole face-reading thing had her squirming under his green-eyed stare.

Maybe it was time to quit modeling. The thought hit her with a force she didn't expect. While Lauren and Paul talked, Sam's brain traveled down a path she hadn't dared to go.

If she left modeling, what were her career choices? She didn't know how to do anything else. The money she'd saved would carry her for several months, but after that? The trust she'd established gave her parents a small amount every month. She'd set that up from guilt over the tremendous sacrifice of time and money by her parents until she was eighteen. If she quit, that income stream for her parents would go away.

She was trapped. Not just by some stupid stalker, but by her lifestyle.

"What's wrong?" Logan couldn't take Mandy's sad face and longing looks toward the house next door.

"I knocked on Sam's door and she didn't answer."

"She's probably busy."

"Doing what?"

Logan shrugged. "How should I know? She's on vacation, remember? Maybe she went sight-seeing." He still hadn't decided what he'd do about his discovery that Samantha Jensen, supermodel, and Vera Samuels might be the same person. He needed more research to confirm.

Ten years after his divorce from Vivian, he'd finally gotten over his disdain for models. Vivian had been a mistake. Except for Mandy. That was the only good thing that came from their union.

Mandy sank onto a lounger and examined her fingernails. "Do you think she'll come with us to help with your class reunion?"

Logan regarded his daughter over the tops of his glasses. "I never agreed to do that."

"Oh, come on, Dad. It'll be fun. One of the girls who plays lacrosse said her mom was going. Please?"

Logan exhaled through his nose. The thought of going anywhere near his old high school peers filled him with anxiety. He'd probably break out in hives. He wiped at the sweat forming on the back of his neck.

"High school wasn't my best era." That was the understatement of the year. Logan still shuddered remembering the feeling of helplessness of being trapped in the janitor's closet. That and the time he clogged the toilet in the restroom, earning him the nickname Log Jam.

Mandy leaned forward, her voice earnest. "You can show them up now, Dad. Look at how successful you are." Mandy's gaze traveled from his head to his bare feet. "A few new clothes and you'll be awesome."

"What's wrong with my clothes?" Logan protested.

"Seriously? You're wearing cargo shorts."

"What's wrong with cargo shorts?"

"What *isn't* wrong?" Mandy snapped her fingers. "I know, let's ask Sam to help find you some cool clothes. She works in the fashion industry."

"I don't think—"

"First thing tomorrow, I'm going to go ask her. I hope she's back by then. Wherever she went."

Logan closed his laptop. "Want to go for a sail? We still have a couple hours before dusk."

"Okay."

Despite Mandy's lack of enthusiasm, Logan refused to let it dampen his enjoyment of something he loved. The gentle rocking of the boat and the crisp scent of lake water filled his senses, grounding him in the present moment. He was aware of his tendency to get too absorbed in projects, but gliding across the sparkling blue waters of Skaneateles always had a calming effect on him. The sun's rays danced and sparkled on the surface, while a light breeze carried the sound of chirping birds and distant boat engines. As they cut through the water, Logan felt a sense of peace wash over him, grateful for this escape from his busy mind.

The wide-open space of the lake helped him relax.

Chapter 11

Sam's phone buzzed early the next morning with a text from her bestie.

Kayleigh: Want to FaceTime?

Sam struggled to a sitting position. Her head pounded and her mouth was stuffed with cotton.

Sam: Give me ten minutes.

Enough time to brew a cup of coffee and wash some of the yuck from her mouth. She'd buried herself in a bed cocoon after Lauren and Paul left, gorging on potato chips, Coke, and another sleeve of Oreos while binging on a Hallmark marathon.

She'd ignored Mandy's rapping on the French doors late in the afternoon, preferring to sink into her pity party. Especially after throwing up all the garbage food.

Carrying a mug of black coffee, Sam wandered out to the living room and sank onto the sofa. Kayleigh's call came a few seconds later.

"Hey, girl, what's up?" Sam asked, balancing the phone on one knee.

"You look terrible," Kayleigh said. A frown formed a crease between her eyebrows.

"Thanks. I can always count on you for encouragement."

"What did you do to your hair? You look like one of those Manga characters."

Sam ran a hand through the uneven haircut. "I'm incognito."

Kayleigh's eyebrows popped up. "Is the puffiness around your eyes part of your disguise?"

"Welcome to my pity party."

Kayleigh's face wrinkled with concern. "What's going on?"

Sam's eyes burned with tears. She'd cried herself to sleep the night before and her head still hurt. "Everything. I'm stuck here, hiding. I have ugly clothes, I've gained a hundred pounds, and my sister is getting married."

"Slow down, girlfriend. One thing at a time. First, you're hiding because some crazy stalker wants to claim you as his girlfriend."

Sam sniffled. "Yeah."

"Second, what's wrong with wearing your own clothes? Nobody knows where you are. Take a shower, put on some makeup, and wear one of your darling outfits."

"They probably won't fit," Sam wailed, swiping at the tears now coursing down her cheeks.

Kayleigh sucked in a breath and let it out. "I can't

help you there. But I doubt you've gained a hundred pounds, though. Maybe ninety-nine."

Sam smiled through her tears. "Maybe." Sam sipped her coffee and set it on the coffee table. "What's new with you? Any recording contract yet?"

"Ugh. No. You'll never believe what happened." Kayleigh reached for something out of sight from the camera. She brought a bottle of water to her lips and took a sip. "Brace yourself, Sam. This is epic."

Half of Sam hoped her best friend had great news to share about her Nashville singing career. But jealousy filled the other half. Everyone in the entire world except her was having fun. FOMO was real.

Kayleigh ran a hand through her naturally curly red locks. "I told you I've been working at this restaurant bar, right? My manager finally let me have a slot to sing one song at one in the morning. Like, who listens to someone that late. By one, everyone's either drunk or leaving with the evening's hook up."

"Okay, but that's awesome."

"Just wait. Around eleven, he asked me to help reorganize the supply room. It was a mess with expired dry goods, canned stuff all over the place, you name it. After about a half an hour, he left to take care of some drunk guys causing problems in the bar."

Kayleigh took a deep breath. Sam waited for the punchline. Kayleigh's gift of administration and organization was legendary. That she also had a voice like Kelly Pickler was amazing.

"Anyway, I got so into getting the room in shape I totally missed my cue. My one chance, Sam, and I blew it."

Sam used the hem of her T-shirt to wipe her nose. She wasn't the only loser. Somehow Kayleigh's predicament seemed worse than her own situation.

"I'm so sorry, Kay. Will he give you another chance?"

Kayleigh grimaced. "That's where it gets worse. He offered me a job as his restaurant manager." Kayleigh's voice raised to a wail. "I'll never break into the music industry."

Sam formed her face into a sympathetic look. "Sure, you will." Her words were anything but convincing as Kayleigh's eyes filled with tears.

"Great, now we're both a hot mess," Sam said, feeling her eyes burn with tears once again.

"I'm thinking of coming home." Kayleigh's words brought Sam's tears to a halt.

"What? No. Stay there. Show Mr. Restaurant guy how awesome you are behind the scenes, and he'll have to give you another chance."

"I don't know, Sam. Maybe I should give up. Call it quits. Come home with my tail between my legs."

"Stop talking like a loser. You're an amazing singer and super creative song writer. At least give it another three months."

Kayleigh brought a tissue to her nose. "Okay. But you hang in there too."

"I will." They disconnected and Sam took a sip of her tepid coffee. Time to pull herself together. No more wallowing in her pity.

First, a shower. Then some clean clothes. If she could find any. She missed her laundry service available in her apartment building. The housekeeper came twice a week and bundled her clothes for the laundry and dry-cleaning service.

The rental had a washing machine, but the myriad controls looked intimidating.

"Come on, Samantha. You can figure it out." After a shower.

Logan was grateful for Carmen keeping Mandy busy throughout the morning. They'd made several dozen chocolate chip cookies and now Carmen was teaching her to make homemade spaghetti sauce from tomatoes she'd picked up at the farmer's market.

He hoped Mandy would forget about the reunion committee meeting that afternoon. He'd drop her off at lacrosse at one and pray she'd be too tired after running in the humid afternoon air to think about anything except a shower or maybe a dip in the lake.

One could hope, right?

"Here, Dad, I brought you a cookie." Mandy set a warm cookie next to his laptop where he worked at the dining room table.

"Only one?"

Mandy waved toward the kitchen. "There's more."

Logan took a bite and groaned. "Fantastic." Mandy's grin warmed his heart. How had he and Vivian managed to create such an amazing daughter? Much of the credit went to his ex, as crazy as she was.

"What are you thinking about? Your face got all weird." Mandy leaned forward and rested her chin on one hand.

"I was thinking how proud I am of you."

Mandy's face flushed. "Aw, Dad."

"I'm serious. You amaze me."

"Are you amazed enough to let me skip lacrosse today?"

"Not that amazed. Get your stuff, and we'll leave in five minutes."

Mandy scooted her chair back and stood. "Don't forget we have a committee meeting this afternoon."

He hadn't forgotten. Three o'clock loomed like a deadline he'd rather not think about. The last time he'd seen his classmates was graduation night. One of his geek friends forced him to go to the grad party at the community center. Worst. Night. Ever.

Not only did the girls turn their backs when he and Gunther stepped into the room, the guys openly mocked them. Their clothes, their hair, even their shoes.

"Hey, Log Jam, wanna see what's in the janitor's closet?" The rough and mocking voices still had the power to make him squirm. He'd been stuck in the closet so long, he'd had to use the mop bucket to urinate. Somehow that information had gone through the gossip mill, causing laughter when he walked down the halls.

Humiliation still burned.

Why was he going to help with the reunion? Because his daughter wanted to help. She thought it would be fun. Thank the good Lord Mandy hadn't had to face the same kind of rejection. Logan made sure she had a generous clothing allowance and enough ready cash to go for ice cream after school. Or to join a club. All things denied him because of his father's addiction.

The only bright spot was he'd be able to spend time with Vera. Or Sam. Or whoever his next-door neighbor was pretending to be.

Mandy bounced out of the house after lacrosse, hair still wet from the shower. "Ready to go, Dad?"

Logan tried to muster enough enthusiasm to answer. "Yes."

"Great. I'll run next door and see if Sam's ready."

Mandy's long legs ate up the distance between the two houses. His home sat at the lower end of a rise. His deck reached to a few feet from the lake's edge. The rental next door was at the top of the hill, looking down. He'd have preferred to be higher, but the house he'd purchased first was more spacious. Perfect for a growing family, should he decide to remarry and have more children.

The way it looked, though, that wasn't in his future. Aside from Mandy forcing him to go to this stupid committee meeting, he rarely left the house, preferring the company of his computer and his housekeeper. Safe. Comfortable.

While waiting for Mandy to return, Logan retrieved his binoculars and studied the houses cozied up to the lake. He'd heard a rumor Derek Jeter, the baseball player, had a home on Lake Skaneateles, but he'd yet to catch a glimpse of the former baseball player. Or any of the supposed famous people who allegedly owned homes here.

He spied Mandy clomping down the outside stairs from the house next door. He quickly shoved the binoculars into their case and laid them on a chair out of sight. Mandy teased him about his obsession with celebrities. He couldn't help it. Their facial expressions fascinated him. When they pranced across the red carpet at some event, often their faces told him they'd rather be someplace else. And with someone other than the woman or man on their arm.

Sam's face told a different story. She'd shown fear when he'd shoved the *People* magazine at her. Why? If she were, indeed, Samantha Jensen, why would she chop off her hair and dye it and hide behind clothes better suited for an eighty-year-old grandma?

Several scenarios came to mind, but the one that made the most sense was obvious. If Vera and Sam were the same person, she was probably hiding from an abusive boyfriend. It must be bad if she was willing to change her appearance so drastically and drop out of sight.

What should he do with his hypothesis?

Chapter 12

By the time Mandy showed up at the back door, Sam was ready to go anywhere just to get out of the house. Boredom and loneliness were in equal measure. If she didn't go somewhere soon, she'd be tempted to order more junk food from the local grocery store delivery service and binge on very unhealthy choices.

Checking herself in the bathroom mirror, Sam convinced herself no one could possibly recognize her without makeup. Her eyebrows and eyelashes faded into nothingness and with a baseball cap pulled low over her uneven hair, not even her mom would recognize her.

Sam enjoyed Mandy's chatter as she followed the teen down the steps and over to her house. Mandy stopped and leaned toward her and whispered, "My dad is, like, always watching through his binocs. He thinks I don't know, but he's trying to spy on, like, famous people."

Sam filed away that bit of information. "That

doesn't sound creepy at all."

Mandy giggled. "I know, right?"

Sam stepped onto Mandy's deck and looked Logan up and down.

"The nineties called, and they want their cargo shorts back."

Mandy laughed. "I told you, Dad."

"What's wrong with them?"

Sam smothered a laugh. "What isn't wrong?"

Logan's cargo shorts hung loosely to his knees. He wore black socks pulled up his calves and black sneakers with Velcro straps.

"Don't be surprised if the fashion police capture you the minute you step out your front door."

Sam grinned at Logan's discomfort.

"Maybe I should stay home."

"No, Dad. You're not getting out of it that easy." Mandy turned to Sam. "I told Dad he should let you pick out some new clothes for him, since you're in the fashion industry and stuff."

Sam chewed on her lip and studied the man. The guys she knew wore the latest designers and knew how to throw together an outfit that didn't make them look like a middle-aged geek. Logan had to be in his mid-thirties. Way too young to look like a Boomer.

"Sure. If this meeting gets out in time, we'll see what good old Lake Skaneateles has in the way of boutiques."

Mandy pumped her fist. "Yes!" She grabbed her

dad's arm and dragged him into the house. "Let's bounce."

Sam followed and skidded to a stop inside the back door. "Wow." Their house was a lot larger than the one she was staying in. Vaulted ceilings rose to a second floor. A grand staircase on one side of the family room fanned out, inviting one to run a hand over the polished wood bannisters. The balcony traversed the room with several doors leading to what she assumed were bedrooms.

"Your house is beautiful," Sam said.

Logan had turned toward her, a disgruntled look on his face. He was probably upset over Mandy and her harsh judgement of his outfit.

"Thanks," Mandy said. "It is pretty cool. But you should see our apartment in the City."

A mansion on the lake, an amazing apartment, and a guy who dressed like an old man. Who was Logan? She'd have to get his last name and do a little web search.

Mandy had said her dad created some software something. And sold it. How much of Mandy's talk was exaggeration? It might be worth checking this guy out.

Not that she was interested or anything. But it would be something to occupy her time when she was alone.

Logan didn't wait for Mandy and Sam to follow

him to the garage. He climbed into his car and pulled onto the driveway so the girls could get in more easily. His ego still smarted from Sam and Mandy's harsh comments. Words from past hurts echoed in his brain.

Look at the loser. Think he shops at Walmart?

Goodwill is more like it.

Hey, Log Jam, the homeless shelter called. They want their clothes back.

If Mandy hadn't been so insistent, he'd have stayed home where he was safe.

Logan fastened his seatbelt and waited for Sam to climb in. Her scent wafted toward him in the close confines of the car. Something fresh, yet exotic. Like the plumeria flowers that grew in Hawaii.

Sam ran a hand over the tan leather seat. "Is this an Aston Martin DB11?"

Logan sent her a sideways glance. "You know cars?"

"I know an expensive one when I see it."

How did a fashion assistant know about the cost of an imported vehicle?

"This is indeed, the Aston Martin DB11. There's nothing like the power of the 528-hp twin-turbo V8 engine of this vehicle. Well worth the quarter mil it costs."

Mandy leaned forward and spoke through the space between the driver and passenger seats. "Stop it, Dad. You're embarrassing me."

"What'd I say?"

Mandy frowned. "My friend, Ainsley from lacrosse is going to be there with her mom. Dad, do you know her mom?"

"What's her last name?"

"Oh. I don't know."

"How many were in your graduating class?" Sam asked.

"About a hundred."

Mandy leaned forward again. "Where did you go to school, Sam?"

Logan glanced sideways and noticed the tension in Sam's jaw.

"Hornell."

"Did you go to your junior and senior proms?"

"No. I couldn't."

"Why?"

Logan caught his daughter's eye in the rearview mirror. "Don't be so nosy, Mandy."

Mandy crossed her arms and sat back with a huff.

"It's okay," Sam said. She turned in her seat. "I had a difficult time with a normal school schedule."

"Were you, like, held back?"

Sam's smile was lopsided. "Not exactly. I had to get a job. I didn't graduate, but I got my GED."

"So you didn't get to go to all the proms and dances and stuff?"

"Sadly, no."

"That stinks. Maybe you and my dad can go to the reunion together?"

Logan tensed. He was only going to this one meeting to mollify his daughter. After today, he'd be done. He had no intention of attending the reunion. And definitely not with Vera or Sam or whoever this woman was sitting next to him.

He pulled into a parking spot at the community center and sucked in a breath. Mandy was already out of the car, bouncing up and down.

"Hurry up, Dad."

Sam didn't look any more excited that he felt. She pulled down the brim of her ball cap.

"I guess that's our cue," Sam said. She climbed out at the same time he did.

Logan watched Sam run her palms down the legs of her polyester pants. If she was hiding, this wasn't a good idea for her to be seen in public. Although Samantha Jensen and Vera Samuels had very little resemblance to each other. Without makeup, she was still beautiful. But why would anyone suspect Samantha Jensen, supermodel, of attending something so nondescript as a high school class reunion planning meeting?

They walked together to the building, Mandy leading the way. Logan breathed a sigh of relief that Sam wore flip flops. She already exceeded his height by four inches.

"Hurry up, guys," Mandy said, waving her hand from the door.

Why did he feel like he was going to his own

funeral?

Approximately a dozen women stood in the meeting room in groups of three and four. One woman wearing tight yoga pants and a tank-type workout top broke away from one of the groups.

"Logan Walters, you haven't changed a bit," she said, grabbing his upper arms.

"Tiffany Skalasky."

She smiled. "It's Bronson now. Remember Bruce?"

Oh, yeah, he remembered Bruce. He was the jock who gave Logan the nickname Log Jam.

Head cheerleader Tiffany and quarterback Bruce were one of the biggest cliches of all time.

"I'm so glad you're here to help. Is this your daughter?" Tiffany turned to Mandy. "My daughter, Ainsley, tells me you're pretty good at lacrosse."

Mandy blushed without answering.

"I'm glad you two are becoming friends."

Ainsley grabbed Mandy's hand and pulled her away. "We're gonna go get snacks from the vending machine."

Tiffany turned a questioning gaze to Sam. "I don't remember you from high school. What year did you graduate?"

Sam held out a hand to shake Tiffany's. "I didn't go to school here. I'm here to help Logan."

Tiffany's gaze swept from Logan to Sam and back. "Oh. Are you two . . ."

Sam recognized the calculating look in the woman's eyes. She moved closer to Logan so that their shoulders touched. Putting her arm around his, she said, "I'm staying here for the summer and thought I'd lend Logan some moral support. I know how difficult it is to be involved in something that could bring back unpleasant memories." She sent Tiffany a saccharine-sweet smile.

She bumped Logan's shoulder with hers and batted her eyelashes. "He's such a workaholic I had to do something to pry him away from his computer." She leaned forward and cupped one hand next to her mouth. "His latest project is very hush-hush. National security."

"Of course." Tiffany spread her arms. "Welcome. We can always use another set of hands."

Sam turned to Logan and winked.

"Let's everyone take a seat," Tiffany said, returning to the front of the room.

At Tiffany's announcement, she and Logan found seats in the back of the room.

"You didn't have to do that," Logan said.

"Ugh. I hate women like that. So judgy."

"You certainly put her in her place."

"You're welcome."

Tiffany spent the next fifteen minutes going through an agenda she projected onto a screen behind her. Sam covered her mouth as she yawned. Why did people think it necessary to read every word of a power point slide when the words were already up there?

"As I mentioned, Penny will join us at the next meeting. She had some medical issues to take care of. We'll need subcommittees for decorations, food, and entertainment. Where are my subcommittee chairs?" Tiffany beamed as three women got to their feet and stood next to her.

"Do you recognize any of them?" Sam asked, leaning over to whisper to Logan.

"Yup. All cheerleaders."

"Figures," Sam said, sliding down on her chair. She hoped they were nicer than Miss Tiffany. Two of the women wore shorts that exposed fleshy thighs and T-shirts that were too tight. The other could have been a Tiffany clone. Tight yoga pants and a workout tank should stay in the gym, in her opinion.

"Which committee do you want to volunteer for?" Sam asked.

"None."

"You think Mandy's going to let you get away with that?"

Logan sat with his arms crossed, clearly uncomfortable. As if conjured up by Sam saying her name, Mandy and her friend Ainsley slid onto seats directly in front of them.

Mandy turned and leaned toward her dad. "Sign up for the decoration committee. It'll be fun. Ainsley told me what her mom is planning."

"It's going to be epic," Ainsley agreed.

"We'll see."

Sam sent Mandy a helpless look and a slight shrug. "I'll do whatever." She was so ready to get out of the house. Even to help with a class reunion for a high school she'd never attended.

Chapter 13

By the time the meeting was over, Logan's plaid cotton shirt was soaked with sweat. Mandy had signed the three of them up to help with decorating the community center ballroom. He grudgingly admired Tiffany's preparation and energy. She'd done a lot of preplanning and was clearly enthusiastic about how successful she expected the event to be.

Mandy's excitement over helping didn't spill over to him. When Tiffany had suggested 'the four of them,' her, Bruce, and Sam should get together for dinner, his stomach threatened to explode. Sam had rescued him, telling Tiffany 'she was keeping him way too busy.' With a wink. A wink! If only he'd known Sam in high school. But she'd probably have been one of the ones to ignore him.

"You ready to go shopping for some new threads, Dad?"

"Uh, no."

Sam pulled a pair of sunglasses from her bag and

put them on. "It'll be fun. You'll see."

Logan sighed. "Fine. Point me in the direction of the mall."

Sam sent him a disgusted face. "Mall? No, no, no. I did a little research and found a cool boutique. I'll send you the pin."

"Awesome," Mandy said, fastening her seatbelt.

Logan punched the address in his GPS, and they set off. Which was worse, shopping for new clothes with his fourteen-year-old daughter and her friend or helping with his high school class reunion. Both made him want to throw up.

"Are you sure we have to do this today? It's getting late."

Mandy piped up from the back seat. "Dad, it's only four thirty."

"Aren't you getting hungry?" Anything to put off this little jaunt.

"I had chips and a Coke at the community center. Besides, we can always grab something on the way home."

Logan glanced sideways at Sam. "What about you?"

Sam shook her head. "I'm okay."

Logan huffed out a breath. "Fine."

Summer days in upstate New York meant the sun would set between nine thirty and ten. He had to admit, they had plenty of time to shop, eat, and still be home in time for a quick sail. He hoped this shopping expedition would be painless.

Sam seemed to sense his angst. "It'll be fun," she said.

"Hmph." Logan preferred ordering from Amazon. No human interaction required.

What seemed like decades later, they climbed into his car, loaded down with shopping bags.

"That wasn't too awful, was it?" Sam asked with a cheeky grin.

Logan pinched his lips together without responding.

Mandy reached forward and patted him on the shoulder. "You did great, Dad. Can we stop and get food?"

Logan's stomach growled. "Sure. But let's get it to go. I'm beat."

"Fine by me," Sam said.

Mandy pulled her phone from her back pocket. "I'll call that Thai restaurant, okay?"

"Sounds good," Sam said. "I love Thai food."

Logan was relieved to let Mandy take care of their order. One less decision he had to make.

"Thanks for letting me hang out with you guys," Sam said. "I was getting cabin fever."

"Why are you here?" The words escaped from his mouth before he could filter them.

"Excuse me?" Sam's hands formed fists on her lap.

"Why are you staying here on the lake, in a rental, for an undetermined length of time?"

Sam's tone changed from friendly to frigid. "That's

none of your business."

Logan was on a roll and couldn't stop himself. "It is my business when you're renting my house."

"You're my landlord?" Sam felt a headache forming behind her eyes. This was not good. As a landlord, he'd be able to force his way in at any time. How would she stay out of sight with him butting in anytime he felt like it?

Sam's phone pinged with a text.

Skyler: He's at it again. Two more letters came today.

Sam typed out a quick response. Did you open them?

Skyler: Yes. Not good. Please stay safe. Taking them to PD.

Sam sent a thumbs up emoji. The hungry growl in her stomach turned to acid. What had the stalker said that was so scary? Would she rather know or not?

Logan's voice broke into her thoughts. "You okay?"

Sam dropped the phone into her purse. "Yeah. Fine."

"You don't look fine. Your face turned white, then green."

"I said I'm fine." Sam didn't mean to sound harsh, but she didn't need Logan digging into her crisis. Mandy set her phone on the seat next to her and leaned forward.

"Food's ordered. Should be about twenty minutes."

The thought of food brought bile crawling up Sam's throat. She shouldn't have gone out in public today. What if someone recognized her and passed the information on to someone in the media?

Until the stalker was caught, she was a prisoner. In a house owned by Logan.

Could this day get any worse?

After a quick stop to pick up the to go order, they arrived back at Logan's house.

Logan stopped his car on the curved driveway of his home to let her and Mandy out. Mandy carried the bag with the food. What should have made Sam's stomach growl and her mouth water instead made her want to hurl.

"I'm going to head home," Sam said.

Mandy halted on her way to the front door. "But I ordered tons of food."

"I'm sorry. I don't feel well." Sam didn't wait for Mandy's response. She strode to the street and headed to her own front door. She unlocked it, stepped in, and closed it behind her before Logan climbed out of his car.

She rushed to the French doors facing the deck and double-checked to be sure they were locked. In the basement, she also checked the door leading outside onto the lake shore.

Satisfied the house was safe, Sam returned upstairs to take a long, hot shower.

The shower head released a pulsing spray over the pebbled shower floor. Sam turned the control all the way to HOT and waited for the water to heat.

And waited.

Where was the hot water? She ran her hand under the spray with a groan of frustration. Still tepid.

"Okay, I'm waiting two more minutes and if it doesn't get hot, I'm going to scream."

She didn't scream. She turned off the water and stamped her foot.

"Why?" she said to the ceiling.

She had two choices. Call the rental agency. Or go next door to the owner. Logan. Why hadn't she gotten his cell number? Or Mandy's.

Sam gritted her teeth and stepped outside into the humid air. She stomped over to Logan's deck and rapped on the sliding glass door.

Mandy appeared a moment later holding a fork. "Did you change your mind?"

"No. I need to talk to your dad."

Mandy's smile faded. "Oh. Okay."

Sam followed the girl into the house, admiring again the beautiful architecture and tasteful decor. A random thought flitted through her head. *How could someone with no fashion sense have such a nice home?* Professional decorators, that's how.

Sam waited just inside the door until Logan approached.

"Mandy said—"

"I have no hot water," Sam said without preamble.

"Huh?"

"Water. Shower. Not there." She waved an impatient hand.

"You don't have hot water?" Logan rubbed a hand over his mouth.

"That's what I'm trying to tell you!" Sam didn't mean to raise her voice, but she was tired, sweaty, and terrified.

"Let me get my tools." Logan swung around and headed deeper into the house.

Sam shifted from one foot to the other, deciding whether to stay and wait for him or return to her place. While she waited, Mandy walked toward her with a bag.

"Here's some Pad Thai in case you get hungry later." She held the bag aloft.

"Thanks." Delicious smells wafted from the to go container. Sam hadn't had Pad Thai in ages. All those carb-filled noodles were not a part of her strict diet. Maybe she'd eat a few later. After a hot shower. If that was in her future.

Chapter 14

"Perhaps I should give you my cell number," Logan said as they traipsed from his home to the rental.

"Perhaps you should."

Logan glanced sideways at Sam. Her gait was stiff and her shoulders hunched. What was going on? Was she so much of a diva that a cold shower had her twisted into a knot?

He stepped into his rental and let out a low whistle. Her living room looked like someone had ransacked it searching for something hidden.

"What happened here?" he asked.

Sam glanced around the room and shrugged. "So, I'm a slob."

She sounded defensive. Logan let it go. "I'll go down to the basement and check the water heater." He really should get the thing replaced. The pilot light had a tendency to go out from time to time.

Sure enough, that was all it was. He climbed back

up the stairs to find Sam staring out the French doors and biting a thumbnail. Even with that choppy haircut, she was beautiful. He'd seen photos of the model, Samantha Jensen, wearing makeup and her hair cascading over her shoulders. But standing in the waning sunlight, with no makeup, and a pair of sweats, this woman took his breath away. He was more than convinced Vera Samuels and Samantha Jensen were the same person. Could she possibly be interested in someone like him?

He allowed himself a moment to fantasize before reality smacked him. Not likely.

"It's fixed. Give the water heater twenty minutes to warm up."

"Okay. Thanks." She turned a distracted look toward him.

"Are you all right?" Logan crossed the room to stand beside her.

"Not really."

"Anything I can do?"

Sam's shoulders drooped. "No."

Logan's heart clenched as a single tear dripped down her cheek. He reached out an arm and laid it stiffly on her shoulder. Tears were his undoing.

"Look, I know we don't know each other well, but maybe I can do something?"

Sam turned toward him, face scrunched into a stiff mask. "It's complicated."

"Tell you what. Let's go out on my boat. I find

being out on the lake clears my head. What do you say?"

Sam inhaled and blew out the breath. "I don't know."

"Come on," Logan urged. "You have to wait for the water to heat up anyway."

Sam chewed her lip. "Okay."

"Great. Meet me on my dock in five minutes." Logan bounced out the door and down the steps to his home. He found Mandy in her room, immersed in her iPad.

"Want to go for a sail with me and Sam?"

Mandy barely spared him a glance. "No thanks."

Logan's disappointment was short-lived. He'd get to spend time alone with Sam. As his daughter would say, he was 'crushing' on their next-door neighbor.

He changed into a pair of his new shorts and out to the boat to get it ready to hit the open water. This was the best part of the day. All the partyers were back on shore, firing up their barbecues and cracking open beers. The lake would be peaceful and hopefully with enough wind to propel *Small Fry* to the middle of the narrow lake. He'd grabbed his binoculars from the storage box and stowed them safely in a waterproof compartment.

Logan couldn't keep his eyes off Sam as she crossed her deck and stepped lightly down the stairs. She'd changed into a pair of shorts and a cropped T-shirt. He admired her long legs and graceful gait as she walked toward him.

"Permission to come aboard," she said, stopping on the deck next to the boat.

"Permission granted." Logan held out a hand to help her climb in. "Grab that rope off the cleat."

Sam complied, and he backed the boat up using the motor. Logan found its low hum relaxing, as if preparing him for complete letdown once he hit open water.

A hundred feet off the shore, he turned off the motor and stood to unfurl the sails.

"Can I help?" Sam asked.

"Sure." Logan explained how to untie the sails and use the rope pulley to release the canvas to the wind. "Not much wind tonight," he said. "But it's still my favorite place to be."

Sam sat in the back of the boat, legs stretched out. She looked completely relaxed, not like back at the house.

"I can see why," she said. "It's like nothing can touch you out here."

The sails barely moved in the stillness. Logan retrieved his binoculars and sat beside her.

"Check this out," he said, handing the glasses to her.

"What am I looking at?" Sam swung the binoculars from side to side.

Logan pointed toward the mansions hugging the shore. "Over there. See the one with the three turrets?

Supposedly the Clintons own it."

"Seriously? Have you ever spotted them?"

"No. But my realtor told me several politicians and other celebrities have homes here on Skaneateles."

Sam let the glasses drop to her lap. "Do you always spy on people when you're out here?"

Logan felt his face warm. "Not always."

"I'm teasing you."

"Oh." He wasn't used to being teased. Bullied, yes. Belittled, yes. Teased, no.

"Nice shorts," Sam said.

"Thanks. Some fashionista helped me pick them out." He sent her a tentative smile.

Sam smiled back. "You have an awesome daughter," she said, handing him the binoculars.

"Thanks. It's all her mother. This will be the first time I've had her longer than two weeks in the summer."

"Why is that?"

"Her mom decided she wanted to move it Italy and didn't want Mandy to go."

"That's rough. I'm glad my parents never got divorced. It's gotta be hard on her."

"It is. And on me, too. I have no idea how to parent a fourteen-year-old."

A gust of wind filled the sails, propelling them forward. Logan jumped up and grabbed the rudder to steer them away from shore.

"We should probably head back. It'll be dark soon."

As they neared the shore, Logan pulled the sails down and anchored them. Before motoring in, he held out his hand. "Give me your phone, and I'll put my information in, so the next time you have a problem with the rental, you can call me."

Sam unlocked her phone. "Why don't you send me a text ,and I'll add you to my contacts."

Logan watched her face as she read her number to him. She'd regained the tight look around her eyes and the firm set to her mouth.

He did as she asked and sent a text to her phone. He heard a ping.

"Got it," Sam said, waving the phone.

Logan concentrated on pulling up to the dock without bumping too hard on the edge. He tied the boat to the mooring cleats and jumped off. Sam grasped his hand as he helped her step onto the deck. She stumbled and he caught her upper arms.

Their faces were inches apart. Logan felt her breath on his cheek. Without thinking, he rose on tiptoes and settled his lips on hers. When she didn't recoil, he increased the pressure to deepen the kiss.

He pulled away and whispered, "Your secret is safe with me."

Sam jerked from Logan's grasp. "What?"

Logan looked like she'd slapped him. "I'm sorry. That shouldn't have happened."

Sam hadn't regretted his kiss. That had been nice. But what he'd said about her secret . . .

"My secret?" Sam put her hands on her hips.

Logan took a step back. "I know who you are. Samantha Jensen."

His words took the air from Sam's lungs. She bent over, trying to catch her breath. Stress and the lack of food had her woozy and lightheaded.

"Let me help you," Logan said, taking her arm and steering her to his deck. Sam let herself be shoved into a chair.

She leaned over, waiting for her head to stop spinning. Logan thrust a bottle of water in her direction.

"Take a drink," he ordered.

"H-how did you know?" Sam asked.

Logan sank onto a chair next to her. "I read faces. I helped create the software for facial recognition used in airports overseas."

Sam slowly raised upright and stared into his unblinking gaze. "You can't tell anyone. Please."

"Why are you hiding?"

Sam chugged down some water and set the half-empty bottle on the wood deck. "I'm being stalked. My manager wants me to lay low until they find him."

Logan nodded.

"You can't say anything to anyone. Including Mandy," Sam said.

"I won't."

Sam believed him. If it was anyone else, they'd be

excited to run to one of the tabloids with the headline 'Supermodel Samantha Jensen in hiding from crazed stalker.'

"Can't tell Mandy what?"

Sam and Logan's heads swiveled to face Mandy. She stood in the doorway with a puzzled look on her face.

Logan stood. "Tell Mandy Sam got a little motion sick on the boat."

Mandy's face scrunched. "Oh, sorry. That happens to me sometimes."

Sam sent Logan a grateful look. "I better get home. Thanks for the sail."

"I'll walk you back." Logan helped Sam to her feet.

She leaned on his arm, grateful for the support. Her legs felt like they belonged to someone else. They reached Sam's back door leading onto the deck. She turned.

"Thank you. For the sailboat ride. And for keeping my secret."

Logan stared down at his feet. "I'm sorry. For the kiss."

Sam's mouth tilted up with a ghost of a smile. "I'm not."

She left him standing there as she went into the house and locked the door. He turned and was soon out of sight. His feet clomped hollowly on the wood steps until there was silence.

Sam wrapped her arms around her middle. What a

day. From pretending to be Logan's girlfriend in front of the 'mean girls,' to shopping, to Skyler's alarming text. All ending with a burned-out water heater, a beautiful late afternoon sail, and a kiss.

And what a kiss. For a nerdy dad, he was an amazing kisser. Sam touched her lips as if she could capture the feeling of his lips on hers and hold it there.

She floated to the bathroom and was gratified to have hot water pouring from the shower head down to the pebbled shower floor.

Like Scarlett O'Hara, she'd think about the stalker situation tomorrow.

Logan slapped his forehead as he almost stumbled down the stairs. What was he thinking? That kiss hadn't been planned. Women like Samantha Jensen didn't kiss men like him. When she'd said she didn't regret the kiss, she was only being polite.

Right?

Logan shuffled to his back deck and sank onto a chair. The waning sunlight cast a glow over Lake Skaneateles. A few stars appeared, forcing their way through the rapidly falling darkness. Except for a distant barking dog, no sounds echoed over the water. The dog quieted.

He was alone. But this time, his aloneness felt scratchy, like a wool sweater on bare skin. First Mandy had invaded his self-imposed prison, forcing him to interact with someone other than his housekeeper, Carmen. Then Sam moved in next door and pulled him further from his comfort zone.

A few weeks ago, he would never have agreed to go shopping in a brick-and-mortar store. And he for sure would not have dared kiss a woman as beautiful as super model Samantha Jensen.

Part of him wanted to crawl back into his shell. He pictured himself as a box turtle, startled and pulling his head as far in as it would go.

The other part wanted to explore these strange new sensations. Could there be a Logan 2.0?

Fat chance, Log Jam.

Voices from his past cut through his self-esteem. Even his dad had looked at him with disdain.

"You'll never amount to anything."

Despite his successful creation and sale of a billion-dollar software product, Logan couldn't shake the feeling of inadequacy brought on by his father's constant criticism. As he looked up at the endless expanse of stars, Logan couldn't help but feel insignificant in comparison to the vastness of the universe.

He'd never given much thought to a Divine creator, but staring up, he thought he might be convinced of its existence. He dared utter a prayer.

"God, if you're up there, help me . . . help him what? Logan had no idea what to ask for. Help him have a relationship with Sam? Help him be a good dad

to Mandy?
The sky held no answer.

Chapter 15

Sam woke to clouds obscuring the morning sun. She sipped her coffee and stared out the French doors at the wind whipping tiny, white-covered waves on the lake. Not a good day to be outside. But a great day to take stock of her life.

First to figure out how to deal with the stalker. Hiding out here seemed to be a solution, but Sam's inactivity was slowly sucking the life from her. She needed people. Logan and Mandy weren't enough to fill her need. Going with them to help Logan's reunion committee was a welcome distraction and still would keep her identity hidden.

Second, time to stop gorging on unhealthy food. The direct correlation between how she felt and what she was stuffing in her mouth was enough to make her stop.

Third and last, Logan. His kiss set something in motion. Could it be time to step away from the limelight and pursue a relationship? That was only possible if she either cut back on her modeling career or quit entirely. But if it didn't work out with Logan, how difficult would it be to step back into modeling?

And what about her parents? They depended on her to supplement their income.

"Grr." Sam chugged down the rest of her lukewarm coffee and slammed the mug on the dining room table. Dirty dishes and the take-out container from the night before littered the room. Clothes she'd taken off were tossed randomly on the furniture. Where was housekeeping when she needed them?

Sam wrinkled her nose at the mess. Someone was always around to pick up after her. Until now. Was she so spoiled she was incapable of picking up after herself? Apparently so.

Mandy's insistent rapping on the French door pulled Sam away from the task of straightening up.

"I want to go paddle boarding, but Dad won't let me go alone." Mandy's voice was breathless like she'd run from her house to here. "He's on a conference call. Will you go with me? Please?" Mandy folder her hands together in supplication.

"I don't know how to paddle board." Sam looked over Mandy's shoulder to the clouds. "Besides, isn't it too windy?"

"It's perfect. Not too hot. And it's supposed to clear up in a half hour. My dad checked his weather app. Please come. I'm dying of boredom."

Mandy looked so pitiful that Sam couldn't help but

smile. "Okay, but I warn you, I've never tried it."

"Go get your swimsuit on. I'll wait here." Mandy plopped down on one of the loungers and pulled out her phone. Sam watched her for a minute. What would it have been like to have a normal high school experience?

She'd been yanked out of school so many times it was impossible for her to graduate with her class. If it weren't for Kayleigh and Lauren and their friend Mike, she would have never survived working and school. Sam still harbored resentment toward her mom for forcing her to model before she'd matured emotionally. Maybe that's why forming relationships with men was so difficult.

Mandy looked up to see Sam still standing in the same spot. She made an impatient gesture. Sam got the message and hurried into the bedroom to change.

Despite falling several times into the cool lake water, Sam finally gained her confidence on the paddle board. Her natural grace enabled her to gradually stand and use the paddle to propel herself forward.

"You're doing it!" Mandy yelled. "Let's race to the platform."

Sam spied a diving platform several hundred yards away. "You're on."

Wind pushed her hair back and raised goosebumps on her damp skin. Gliding over the water under her own power felt amazing. This was one of the things she'd missed during her unusual teen years. Sam added it to the mental list of lost opportunities.

Group dating, school dances, football games, all normal part of high school. As an adult, she couldn't capture those times. But the simple act of pushing herself on the paddle board brought grateful tears to her eyes. It felt like freedom.

Freedom from the relentless grind of posing for the camera or on the runway. Freedom from keeping up appearances with movie stars and musicians. Freedom from having to look perfect when she stepped out of her apartment.

With no makeup and sopping wet hair, Sam felt as if a weight had been lifted from her shoulders.

Logan's heart swelled with pride as he watched his daughter and Sam glide effortlessly through the water towards the diving platform. He couldn't help but feel a tinge of guilt as he used the binoculars to zoom in on Sam's lithe form. She moved like a creature of pure grace, her body undulating with each powerful stroke. Logan couldn't tear his gaze away from her, mesmerized by the way she seemed to cut through the water like a swan. Every movement was precise and fluid, her slender arms pushing the paddle of the board over the waves with ease. As he watched, he couldn't shake off the feeling there was something special about Sam, something that set her apart from everyone else. Not simply her outward beauty.

No wonder someone was stalking her. He'd keep her secret and protect her if need be.

The girls reached the diving platform and jumped off the paddle boards into the lake. Their shrieks carried over the surface to where Logan stood on his deck. What would happen when he returned to New York City, and Mandy went back to school? Would his daughter want to continue her friendship with Sam? How would that work? He'd be forced to come into contact with Sam.

While that sounded good on the surface, he was not comfortable with the way he was so strongly attracted to Sam. There was no way she felt the same attraction. Simply not logical a super model would be attracted to a software geek. Especially with his disability. Not even Mandy knew how far he was on the autism spectrum. Psychologists called it Asperger's, but that term was slowly morphing into 'on the spectrum.'

Vivian had put up with his focus and obsessions until she ran out of patience. Once her modeling career took off, she didn't need him. Logan had secretly been relieved when she'd moved into an apartment with a male friend—until Logan found out she was pregnant with his child. After that, she'd quit modeling and moved from friend to friend, some male, some female. How Mandy had turned out so well was still a mystery.

Shouts from the diving platform snapped Logan from his thoughts. Mandy waved to him from where she stood on the platform. She cupped her hands around her mouth and shouted, but Logan couldn't make out the words.

He raised the binoculars to his eyes and focused on her dripping form. Mandy waved at him to join them. Should he?

Before he could second-guess his decision, Logan ran to the end of the pier and dove into the water. He came up gasping at the chill. His muscles warmed as he swam toward where his daughter stood, cheering him on.

"Come on, Dad, you can do it!"

Logan reached the edge of the platform and grabbed onto the sodden planks with one hand, using the other to push his hair from his eyes. He made his way around to the side and used the ladder to pull himself onto the platform.

Goosebumps rose on his arms. "That's cold."

Sam lay back, resting her weight on her arms. She lifted her face to the sky where the sun had broken through the clouds. "Yes, it is. But the sun feels good."

Logan let his eyes roam over her stretched-out form. The one-piece swimsuit fit her like a second skin. Desire caused his pulse to speed up. He looked away, focusing instead on the other people on the platform.

A dad with two kids made eye contact and nodded. Logan nodded back and turned his attention to Mandy.

"You two going to stay out here all day?" Logan asked.

Sam glanced at Mandy. "I'm ready to head back

whenever you are."

"What time is it, Dad?" Mandy asked.

"It's about lunch time."

"Cool. I'll eat, and you can take me to lacrosse." She lowered her paddle board into the water and straddled it. Grabbing the oar, she started for the shore. "See you at home," she called over her shoulder.

Logan watched her head toward their pier. "I'm glad she's enjoying lacrosse. I thought she'd want to quit by now."

Sam stood to face him. "She hates lacrosse. That's not why she's excited to go."

"What are you talking about?"

"Remember her friend, Ainsley, from the reunion committee meeting? Tiffany's daughter? Ainsley has a brother."

"And?" Logan tried to gather the threads of this conversation.

Sam rolled her eyes and shoved his shoulder. "Ainsley's brother, Daxton, is sixteen. He takes Ainsley to practice every day and stays to watch the girls play."

Logan locked eyes with Sam, letting this new information click into place.

"Oh."

Sam shoved the paddle board into the water. "Yeah, oh." She jumped off the platform feet first.

"Wait. Should I be worried?" This was troublesome. His daughter was interested in a boy? He was not ready for his new development.

Sam mounted the board and reached out. "Hand me the oar, please."

Logan did and watched as she dipped the paddle into the water. "I wouldn't worry. Yet."

The urge to dive in and swim alongside her. Instead, he sat on the edge of the platform and digested Sam's comment. What did she mean by 'yet'?

Chapter 16

Sam almost laughed at Logan's expression. It was a combination of terror, confusion, and angst. Even if Ainsley's brother took an interest in Mandy, once they all went back to school, that would be the end of any summer romance.

Still, at fourteen, Mandy was too young to date. Unless things had changed since she was a teen. Not that her teen years were normal. There was never enough time for dating.

Sam focused on the rhythmic dip of the paddle in the water, propelling her toward Logan's dock. Mandy was already there, pulling her board onto the deck and stowing her paddle.

"Let me help you," Mandy said.

Sam lowered herself to a sitting position and handed the paddle up to Mandy's waiting hands. She slid sideways until she could scoot onto the deck without having to use the ladder.

"That was fun," Sam said, reaching for a towel.

"What time do you have to leave for lacrosse practice?"

"I almost forgot," Mandy said. "Pretty soon, I guess."

"What do you like best about lacrosse?" Sam pasted an innocent look on her face.

Mandy blushed. "I, uh …"

"Daxton?"

"Well—"

Mandy was saved from answering when Logan pulled himself up on the dock. Sam let her eyes rove over his dripping form. No one would call him handsome in the traditional sense, but Logan was easy on the eyes.

Stop it, she told herself. You are not allowed to be attracted to someone you'll never see again after you leave.

But she was. Logan represented normal. He wasn't attached to the fashion industry, nor to any celebrity status. Despite his awkwardness, Logan was a good dad. Sam was sure she could trust him not to tell anyone who she was and where she was. Logan was safe.

Sam reached for a pile of folded towels and handed one to Logan.

"Thanks." He rubbed the towel across his face and used it to push his hair back.

"Turn around," Mandy said.

Sam whirled around. Mandy snapped a photo with her cell phone. "Now I have a picture to put with your name and number."

"Let me see," Sam said, holding out her hand. The photo showed her with eyebrows raised in surprise. Her hair was a glorious mess around her head. "Ugh," she said, handing the phone back to Mandy.

"I'm gonna go change," Mandy said.

"She's a good kid," Sam said, turning back to Logan.

"Thanks. I'm surprised she's turned out as well-adjusted as she has. Her mom, well, she hasn't been the best role model."

Sam waited for Logan to say more, but he seemed unwilling to trash his ex-wife. Good on him.

"I better get back and change out of this swimsuit." Sam made a move to go, but Logan stopped her.

"Thanks for being a friend to Mandy. I appreciate it. She needs more female role models."

Sam smiled into his green eyes. "You're welcome."

Logan's gaze locked onto her, as if it had the power to bind her in place. Unspoken energy seemed to flow between them, an invisible thread Sam couldn't quite identify. It was a tantalizing sensation, a spark that felt very much like the pull of attraction.

"I-I better go." Sam broke eye contact and turned to go.

Mandy stuck her head out the back door. "Hey, Sam, when's your birthday?" She held her phone aloft. "I'm putting your info in here."

"Oh, it's, uh, July 4."

"No way! That's next week. Dad, let's have a party."

Logan and Sam spoke at the same time.

"No—"

"I don't—"

Mandy frowned. "Fine. Whatever." She slammed the slider closed.

"Okay, well, bye," Sam said, trying to wrap her head around the last five minutes of her life. She scrambled off the deck and practically ran to her place. When she reached the deck, she turned once to see Logan still standing where she'd left him. Inside the safety of her rental, she locked the door and headed for the shower.

Logan waited until Sam disappeared into his rental before heading inside his own home. Mandy was nowhere in sight. The only sound was Carmen in the kitchen, no doubt making lunch.

He stuck his head in the kitchen. "Carmen, we're going to have to eat quickly before I take Mandy to lacrosse."

"Very good, Mr. Logan. It's ready now." She waved a hand over two plates, each with a sandwich cut diagonally and a handful of sliced carrots.

"Go ahead and put it on the table. I'm going to take a quick shower."

Carmen nodded her agreement.

When Logan returned to the dining room, he found Mandy already at the table, phone in one hand and half a sandwich in the other.

"We will need to leave in thirty minutes," Logan said, consulting his watch.

Mandy grunted in response. She set her sandwich down. Her thumbs raced across the screen.

"Dad, is Sam, like, your girlfriend?"

Logan choked on the bite of sandwich he'd just bitten off. "What?"

"I saw you kissing her. Isn't that something you only do with your girlfriend?"

Logan's brain scrambled for an answer. "I, um, no."

"No, it isn't or no, it is?"

Logan took a sip of water. "I don't want to have this conversation with you."

"I'm not a child, Dad. I want to know if Sam is your girlfriend because I saw you kiss her."

Logan took a deep breath. "Sam is not my girlfriend."

"But you kissed her." Mandy's eyes burned into his.

"Yes, I did. Once."

"So . . ." Mandy's eyebrows rose.

Logan pushed his chair back. "It's time to go." He picked up the plate with his uneaten sandwich and carried it into the kitchen. Behind him, Mandy made a disgusted sound.

"Fine, don't talk to me." Her voice rose. "But if I kiss a boy who isn't my boyfriend, then it must be okay."

Logan had no answer. This single dad of a teenager role did not fit him. Perhaps he could put Mandy on a plane and send her to Italy with her mom.

They drove to the community center in frigid silence. Mandy sat with her arms crossed and a mulish look on her face. Logan tried to engage her, but Mandy refused to answer. When they reached the lacrosse field, she jumped out and slammed the car door closed, despite having been told multiple times not to.

"The Aston Martin is a fine example of excellent craftsmanship," Logan had told her. "The doors are meant to be closed like this." He'd shown her how to gently close the doors without using force.

His jaw tightened as he watched Mandy stride across the grass toward a group of girls. Maybe he'd sit in the car and watch her practice. What had Sam said about Mandy enjoying her friend's brother more than lacrosse?

Logan watched as a boy approached the group of girls. Mandy walked to him and appeared to be holding a conversation.

Logan jumped when someone knocked on his window. Tiffany stood next to his car with a huge smile. He buzzed down the window.

"Logan, hi. I see you're dropping Mandy off for practice."

Was that a question? Was Tiffany waiting for a response?

Tiffany leaned over to bring herself to eye level with him. "We're going to be painting the backdrop for the reunion dance tonight. I hope I can count on you and your girlfriend for help."

Logan swallowed several times before answering. "Okay." That was the best he could come up with. Why was everyone so determined to turn Sam into his girlfriend?

"Let's get our girls together soon. They've become good friends."

"Okay." He sounded like a robot.

Tiffany straightened and waved her fingers. "Bye, bye.

See you at six."

Logan raised the window and slumped down in the seat. He glanced over to where Mandy and her teammates were warming up. She sent him a death glare and waved him away.

Putting the car in drive, Logan pulled out of the parking lot and headed to the safety of his home.

Back at the house, Logan carried his laptop out to the deck. He did his best work outside. Opening a new browser, he started a search for every bit of information he could find on Samantha Jensen.

Chapter 17

After a long shower, Sam rummaged in the refrigerator for something to eat. She sniffed a to go box containing leftover Chinese food and rejected it as too old.

"Peanut butter and jelly," she said aloud. "Always a good standby." Eating bread was a luxury she rarely ate because of the carbs. "I probably worked off the calories on the paddle board."

Sam assembled the sandwich and took a huge bite just as the doorbell rang. A shaft of alarm caused her to drop the sandwich.

"Who could that be?"

A peek through the peephole found her sister, Lauren, standing on the porch holding a travel bag.

"What are you doing here?" Sam asked, swinging open the heavy wood door.

Lauren grinned. "I'm here to keep you company." She waved to a waiting vehicle.

"Who's that?"

"Paul's assistant dropped me off."

"Where's Paul?"

Lauren pushed her way past Sam and dropped her bag. "He had to fly to Colorado to check on one of his care homes. He'll be gone a few days. So, I thought I'd spend some quality time with my sister." Lauren opened her arms for a hug.

Sam let herself be swept into her big sister's comforting arms. She needed this. Lauren could help sort out her life. The growing attraction she felt toward Logan, her delight in getting to know his daughter, and this constant underlying fear that her stalker would somehow discover where she was.

"Want a sandwich?" Sam asked, heading into the kitchen.

"Sure."

Lauren leaned against the middle island while Sam made another sandwich. "I see you learned to cook."

"Very funny. Don't forget who's holding the knife."

"So noted."

"Let's take these outside."

They carried their lunch to the deck and sat on matching loungers. "I'll get us a Diet Coke." Sam returned to the kitchen, filled with gratitude for Lauren. No longer would she have to face this exile alone. She returned to the deck carrying two bottles of soda.

"This is awesome," Lauren said. "I haven't had a chance to relax since we started planning our wedding."

"I love it here. I just wish it were under different

circumstances."

"Speaking of, any movement on finding your stalker?"

"Nope. And I'm super frustrated with Skyler. I feel like she's ignoring me." Skyler's lack of communication was troubling.

Lauren flipped a hand toward Logan's house. "How are things with the kid next door?"

Sam's face grew warm. She shoved a hand through her hair.

"You're taking a long time to answer. What gives?" Lauren asked.

Sam stood and walked to the railing and looked out over the lake. "Something happened." She turned. Lauren pinned her with her gaze.

"I know that look," Lauren said. "It's the same look you had when you and Mike thought you'd end up happily ever after."

Sam's mouth curled up into a half smile. "That didn't work out."

"You better tell me what's going on. This is about the dad, isn't it?"

Sam gave a half-shrug.

"Ooh, Sis. You better get over here and tell me every single detail."

Sam strode to the lounger and plopped down, hugging herself.

What could she say to capture in words the feelings Logan evoked by that one kiss?

"You like him."

"Maybe."

Lauren leaned toward her. "You do! You like him. I need all the tea, Sis."

Sam let out an exasperated sigh. "I don't know, Lauren. I'm worried it's because he's the only male within shouting distance. And because he's so different than anybody I've ever gone out with."

"Because he's a straight, single dad? Sounds perfect."

Sam giggled. "And he's a great kisser."

Lauren dropped her sandwich. "You didn't!"

Sam nodded. "I didn't. He did. And it was amazing."

"Sounds like things are moving along in that situation. What about his daughter?"

"She's adorable. Fourteen and changes from happy to emotional and back within a nanosecond. I'm surprised she's so normal, given that her mom basically dropped her on Logan's doorstep, waved goodbye, and took off with her new husband."

"That's harsh."

Sam took a sip of her soda. "Logan is … quirky. I have a feeling he's on the autism spectrum."

"Does that bother you? I mean, if you were to pursue a relationship, would it make or break the decision?"

"I don't know yet. But wait till I tell you about his high school reunion committee meeting." Sam told

Lauren in great detail about how the women had judged her and Logan because of their clothes, and how she'd put the chairwoman in her place by pretending to be Logan's girlfriend.

"Wait until she finds out who you really are. That'll take the wind out of her sails," Lauren added between hoots of laughter.

"Speaking of sails, I've been out on Logan's sailboat a couple of times." Sam relaxed against the lounger, feeling again the freedom of dancing over the water with the wind on her face. Real wind, not one created by a giant fan. "It was amazing, Lauren."

"You've been on sailboats before. What's the difference?"

"The difference is Logan's boat only seats four people. It isn't a yacht. You're right down on the water."

Lauren's gaze pinned Sam. "You need to think long and hard about whether or not to get involved with this guy."

"Says the woman who's marrying a man after knowing him for ten seconds."

"I mean it, Sam. Are you falling for him or his lifestyle of simplicity? What happens when you go back to work?"

Sam huffed out a breath. "I don't know."

Mandy had hinted that her dad might be wealthy, but so far Sam hadn't seen any evidence of money. Sure, he owned two homes on Lake Skaneateles, but a lot of New Yorkers kept an apartment in the City and a home somewhere else. And he had a very expensive vehicle.

Not many men wanted their significant other to be constantly on display wearing designer clothes or prancing down a runway at a fashion show. Not to mention the cameras lurking around every corner. Sam had to ensure her clothes and makeup were perfect every time she left her apartment. Paparazzi would love to catch the famous supermodel with lipstick on her teeth.

Sam's phone buzzed with a text.

Logan: Painting the backdrop for the reunion today. Can you come?

Sam typed out a response. Sure.

"Hey, Sis, want to go with me and meet the mean girls I told you about?"

Lauren grinned. "Yeah, let's go have some fun."

Logan breathed a sigh of relief at Sam's thumbs-up emoji. He wasn't ready to face the committee women by himself. His phone buzzed again with another text from.

Sam: My sister is coming with us. Hope that's okay.

It was Logan's turn to send the thumbs up. He'd read up on all things Samantha Jensen. She'd begun modeling around the age of fifteen and had built a successful career. She'd been photographed with movie stars, pop stars, and other celebrities through the years but the only ones that sparked rumors of a serious relationship were the ones with Dawson Knox.

Logan's stomach tightened. Of course, someone like Sam would be attracted to a superstar like Knox. He had it all—looks, money, charm, and adoring fans. Logan had money. Full stop. No charm, no looks, and definitely no adoring fans.

Before he could tap out a text telling Sam never mind about the committee meeting, his phone beeped, alerting him it was time to pick Mandy up from practice.

With a groan of frustration, Logan set off for the community center. Which Mandy would climb into his car today? Happy and tired Mandy or cranky and irritable Mandy? His life was becoming too complicated. He longed to go back to the days when he could spend hours immersed in work and only come up for air when Carmen forced him to eat.

He could take his little boat out on the lake and enjoy the solitude. No one criticized his clothing. Nobody pushed him to get involved in outside activities.

Logan pulled up to the community center in time to see Mandy wrap her arms around a boy and give him a hug. He grabbed the door handle, ready to jump out and … do what? Shove the kid to the ground and embarrass his daughter? The hug lasted only a couple of seconds before the boy disentangled himself. Logan wished he had his binoculars so he could read the kid's lips.

Mandy grabbed her water bottle and bounced toward Logan's waiting car.

"Hi, Dad," she said, climbing in. "Thanks for being on time."

"Thanks for setting my alarm." Logan put the car in drive, working on something to say to address what he'd just witnessed. "How was practice?" He cringed at the lame question.

"Great. We have a scrimmage next week against Hornell."

"I ran into Ainsley's mom earlier. She wants to arrange a play date."

He felt Mandy's stare and turned to look.

"Seriously, Dad? A play date? I'm not six."

"Oh, right. I thought …"

Mandy's look of disgust told him he was the dumbest dad in the world. "Ainsley and I are going to hang out later while you're working on the decorations. She invited me over to their house for dinner after."

"Will Ainsley's brother be there?" The words slipped out before Logan could stop them.

Mandy bowed her head over her phone, ignoring his question.

Logan let his question disappear into the hormone-charged air inside his car. Excited Mandy turned into sullen Mandy in a nanosecond.

"Sam will join us too."

No answer.

"And her sister."

This comment brought Mandy's head up. "I met her. She's nice."

Logan had no answer. They rode the rest of the way home in silence. He pulled into the garage and climbed out, feeling unsettled. His daughter had a crush on her friend's brother, and he had a crush on a supermodel.

They were both a hot mess.

Chapter 18

"**Are you ready** for this?" Sam asked as she and Lauren grabbed their purses and headed out the front door.

"So ready. This'll be fun. And a nice break for me from wedding stuff. Mom is driving me crazy with suggestions for food, music, decorations, and where we should go on our honeymoon."

Sam laughed. "I'm glad her attention is on you and not on me."

"Does she know you're in hiding?"

"Nope. And I want to keep it that way."

"You better hope she doesn't read *People Magazine.*"

Logan was already waiting in his driveway with the Aston Martin running. Sam spied Mandy exiting the house, head down as she stared at her phone.

Sam nudged Lauren. "I'm glad we didn't have cell phones when we were that age."

"Agreed."

"Hi, Mandy. You remember my sister, Lauren, right?"

Mandy glanced up. "Sure. Hi."

"Do you want to sit up front with your dad?" Sam asked.

"No, you go ahead."

Sam and Lauren exchanged a look. Sam opened the door and climbed in. The air conditioning blew icy air toward her face.

"Hi," Logan said. "Feel free to adjust the A/C."

"It's fine," Sam said, grateful for the air to cool her cheeks. Logan's closeness brought a flush crawling up her neck. The interior of the car smelled like pine. Was it his aftershave or an air freshener? She resisted the urge to lean closer and sniff him.

"I hope you're wearing something you won't mind getting paint on," Logan said.

Sam turned in her seat to see Lauren's look of dismay. Since meeting Paul, Lauren had begun to shop at exclusive boutiques specializing in clothing for plus-sized women. Her outfit today was from a designer Sam recognized. It probably cost her at least twelve hundred.

"Maybe I'll just supervise," Lauren said, running a hand down her flowered skirt.

"I'm okay." Sam had no worries about ruining her thrift store outfit.

Mandy leaned forward and spoke through the space between the seats. "Yeah, why do you dress like an old lady? I would think since you're in the fashion industry, you'd have a lot better clothing sense."

"Mandy," Logan said. "That's rude."

"Well, she did take you shopping."

Sam covered her mouth. Mandy had no idea about her so-called disguise. She pulled the brim of her ball cap lower. "I guess I could update my wardrobe, eh?"

Before Mandy could respond, Logan pulled into a parking spot at the community center.

"Look, there's Daxton." Mandy couldn't climb out of the car fast enough.

Sam watched Logan's face. His jaw tightened and his knuckles gripping the steering wheel turned white. "It's a harmless summer crush," she said, getting out of the car.

She and Lauren watched as Mandy and the boy hugged.

"Aren't they cute?" Tiffany's voice startled Sam.

"Yeah. Cute." Except Logan looked ready to commit murder. Sam grabbed her sister's arm. "Come on, let's go inside."

Sam introduced Lauren to Tiffany as they walked into the building, Logan on their heels.

Inside the building, Tiffany stopped and held out a hand to shake Lauren's. Tiffany's gaze traveled from Lauren's head to her Manolo Blahnik sandals. Tiffany sniffed, as if Lauren were somehow lacking.

Sam narrowed her eyes. "Lauren recently got engaged." She leaned toward Tiffany and spoke in a loud whisper. "You may have heard of her fiancé, Paul

Montrose. He was on the cover of Forbes a few months ago."

"Forbes?"

Sam almost laughed at Tiffany's look of confusion. "It's a finance magazine. I thought everyone's heard of it. And of Paul. You know, 'Youngest Billionaire.'"

Tiffany's look turned from snobby to calculating. "Of course. Welcome, Lauren, to our little reunion committee."

When Tiffany had wandered off to greet some of the other women, Sam pulled Lauren aside. "She's probably trying to figure out how to weasel her way into your life."

Lauren rolled her eyes. "Not happening."

Logan caught up to them. "What are you two talking about?"

"Nothing important." She sent him a dazzling smile. "Let's get to painting."

Tiffany had set up a wooden plank against one of the walls. Someone had stenciled a design on it, depicting popular cars from the year they graduated.

"Grab a brush and some paint," Tiffany instructed. "Here's a color drawing of what it should look like when it's done." She taped the drawing to the wall next to the plank.

"I guess that's our cue to get started," Sam said. She picked up a brush and a small can of blue paint.

Several minutes later, she turned to see Logan standing in the same spot holding a brush and looking confused.

"Need some direction?" she asked.

"This isn't my forte."

"Come on, loosen up. This isn't rocket science. Dip your brush in the paint and start."

Logan couldn't get his arms to move. Between sitting next to Sam in his vehicle, seeing his teenage daughter hug some boy, and hearing Sam's sister was engaged to *the* Paul Montrose, Logan's senses were on overload.

Sam smelled like fresh strawberries. Standing next to Sam now, her scent wafted toward him. He could barely breathe.

"Is your sister really engaged to Paul Montrose?" Logan stroked the bristles of the skinny brush in one hand.

"Yeah. So?"

"Have you met him? I mean, sure, you probably have."

Sam sent him a sideways glance. "Of course. He's very nice. Why?"

Logan shrugged. "I've read a lot about him."

"I'm sure you have," Sam murmured. "You do read *People Magazine*, after all."

Logan swayed when Sam sent a smile his direction.

"Perfect!" Tiffany said, holding her cell phone like a camera. "This will go on our slide show at the reunion."

Logan's gaze swept from Sam's alarmed expression to Tiffany's smug smile. "Sam doesn't like her picture taken," Logan said, taking a step toward Tiffany.

"I thought you said her name was Vera."

Logan swallowed. "Uh, yeah. Vera."

Sam dropped her brush into a can of rinse water. "My name is Vera Samuels, but everybody calls me Sam."

"How cute." Tiffany pocketed her phone and turned away.

"I'm sorry," Logan said when the woman walked away to examine the work of another person. "Want me to tell her to delete your photo?"

Sam looked down at her paint-splattered hands. "No, it'll be okay. Hopefully by the time your reunion comes around my stalker will be caught."

Logan heard the unspoken words, *and I can go back to my life.*

Lauren approached with a huge smile. "Logan, Tiffany invited Paul and me to come to your reunion when I told her we went to Hornell High."

Sam's mouth dropped open and snapped closed. "You told her what?"

Lauren swept a confused glance from him to Sam. "She asked if we were from around here. Wasn't I supposed to?"

Sam looked ready to explode. So far, Sam had managed to keep her identity secret. But her sister had wiped that away with one innocent statement.

Logan grabbed Lauren with one hand and Sam with the other, dragging them outside to a courtyard. The humid air hit him like a wet sock.

Sam stood with her arms crossed. "Thanks a lot, Lauren. Now Tiffany will do a little digging and discover there was no Vera Samuels who graduated from Hornell High School."

Lauren raised her hands in surrender and let them drop. "You're the one who bragged I was engaged to Paul. It doesn't take a genius to look him up and find our engagement announcement, which includes the detail that my sister happens to be supermodel Samantha Jensen."

Sam put a hand on either side of her head. "Oh my gosh. What am I going to do?"

Chapter 19

Sam looked up from watching the paint swirl from her hands down the sink in the community center restroom. Her paint-dotted reflection stared back.

Stay under the radar, Skyler had said. Lay low.

Instead, she'd let Logan talk her into helping with this stupid committee. Everything would have been fine if Lauren hadn't opened her big mouth and told that woman where they'd gone to high school.

Not all the blame was Lauren's, Sam admitted to herself. She couldn't help putting Tiffany in her place by bragging about Lauren's billionaire fiancé. Well, what's done was done.

Sam dried her hands on the rough brown paper towel and tossed it in the direction of the trash can. It bounced off the rim and onto the floor. She stared at it for a second and walked out of the restroom.

"Take me home," she told Logan. He and Lauren stood outside the community center in a patch of shade.

Lauren reached out to grab Sam's arm. Sam jerked

away.

"I'm sorry, Sam."

"There's nothing to be done about it now."

They drove back to the house in silence. Logan pulled into the driveway and stopped to let her and Lauren out.

"Who's that?" Logan asked, squinting at someone standing at Sam's front door.

Sam stepped out of the car with a flash of alarm. A man held a white packet in one hand and with the other he punched the doorbell.

"Hey," Sam called. The guy swung around to face her. Lauren climbed out of the back seat and stood next to her.

"It's fine," Sam said. Crossing the driveway and stretch of grass separating Logan's house from her rental, she greeted the man. "Frank, what are you doing here?"

Frank shifted his weight from one leg to the other and shoved the packet in Sam's direction. "Skyler asked me to deliver your mail."

Sam noticed the camera hanging around Frank's neck. "Always on duty, eh, Frank?" she teased.

Lauren stepped onto the porch. "Hi. I'm Lauren."

Sam turned to her sister. "Lauren, this is Frank. He's one of our staff photographers. And I guess also deliveryman. Do you want to come in, Frank?"

"Oh, no. I don't want to be a bother. But Skyler asked me to take a picture of you so she knows you're okay."

Sam raised her eyebrows. "Oh, okay. C'mere, Lauren. Let's get Frank to take us both."

Lauren posed next to Sam as Frank stepped back to snap several photos of the two of them.

Sam spied Logan staring from his car. She waved and turned to unlock the front door.

"If you won't come in, at least let me get you a bottle of water."

"Thank you."

Sam unlocked the door and left it open while she retrieved a cold bottle from the fridge. "Here you go. And please tell Skyler thank you."

Frank's head bobbed. "Will do."

She closed the door and found Lauren staring out the French doors.

"Forgive me?" Lauren asked, turning to face Sam.

Sam huffed out a breath through her nose. "Of course. I'm as much to blame as you. But from here on out, I am staying in this house. No more committee meetings, no more shopping, nothing."

Lauren spread her arms and Sam leaned into her embrace. "I'm worried about you, Sam."

"I know. I'm just so tired to being stuck here. I'm trapped."

"Do you have any ice cream?" Lauren asked.

"Of course."

"You go sit, and I'll dish some up."

Sam sank onto the sofa and raged again at her

situation. If her face weren't so well known, she wouldn't have attracted a stalker. If she weren't a model, no one would care what she did. If she quit tomorrow, would the stalker go away?

"What are you thinking about so seriously," Lauren asked, handing Sam a bowl of mint chip.

"Thinking about quitting."

"Because of the stalker?"

"Because all of it. The stalker, the schedule, the lack of personal relationships, lack of control over my life." Sam took a huge bite of ice cream and let it slide down her throat. "Not being able to enjoy a bowl of ice cream."

"What about the glamour? The money? The exciting invitations to red carpet events?"

"That's the problem," Sam said glumly. "I have no skills other than looking good in pretty clothes."

Sam watched as Lauren's gaze swept over the clothes and dishes strewed around the room. "It's obvious you have zero housekeeping skills."

Sam pointed her spoon at her sister. "Exactly. What could I do if I quit? Besides, who would support Mom and Dad?"

Lauren's spoon clattered when she dropped it into her bowl. "What?"

"I guess I never told you I send money to Mom and Dad every month. They sacrificed so much for me growing up. It's the least I can do."

"You cannot let some warped sense of obligation

keep you trapped. If you decide to walk away from your career, Mom and Dad will have to figure it out."

Sam was saved from answering by a text.

Logan: Sorry about today. I'm going to take the sailboat out. Want to come? Lauren too.

"Want to get some fresh air?" Sam asked, setting her empty bowl on the coffee table.

"Where we going?"

"Put on some shorts and a hat and meet me outside in two minutes." Sam sent Logan a thumbs up emoji and told him they'd be there in five minutes.

Sam undressed quickly and slipped into her one-piece swimsuit and oversized T-shirt. She thrust her feet into flip-flops and tapped her foot while waiting for Lauren.

"Hurry up," Sam said as Lauren gathered her hair into a ponytail and threaded it through the space in the back of her baseball cap.

"Nice hat," Sam said, eyeing the Yankee's logo.

"Paul is a huge Yankee's fan. Ready. Now will you tell me where we're going?"

Logan ran his palms down the thighs of his new fashionable shorts. He missed the multitude of pockets in the cargo shorts. Who decided cargo shorts were passé? He'd never be cool, despite new clothes.

But he'd gotten Sam to agree to a sail. He admired her long legs as she sped down the stairs of her deck and ate up the space separating the two houses. His pulse sped up as she neared.

Logan swallowed to moisten his suddenly dry mouth.

Sam stopped a foot in front of him. "Permission to come aboard," she said with a salute.

"Permission granted." Logan stepped aside and held out his hand to assist Sam and her sister into *Small Fry*.

Sam settled herself in the back, and Lauren sat next to her. Logan untied the craft and jumped in after pushing away from the dock.

"Are you ready for some wind?" Sam asked, grinning at her sister.

Logan's breath caught at the sight of Sam's smiling face. Despite wearing a stretched-out tee and no makeup, she was beautiful. Could he dare think she might want to pursue a relationship after she returned to her normal life?

He had nothing except his money to offer. No bright lights or exciting galas, no paparazzi waiting to catch his picture. Boring, steady, content to exist in his safe and comfortable bubble.

Yeah, she'd be gone soon, and he'd be alone again. Except for Mandy. Logan comforted himself with that thought.

As if Sam could read his thoughts, she asked. "Where's Mandy?"

"She's with her friend Ainsley." And probably the girl's brother, Daxton. The thought made his jaw tighten.

Sam leaned forward. "Don't worry about her. She's a good kid. Once the summer is over, they'll go their separate ways."

And so will you. The thought depressed him.

"Want help with the sails?" Sam asked, getting to her feet.

"Sure."

Sam deftly unfurled the sails, and Logan cut off the engine to allow the wind to fill the canvas.

Soon the small boat skimmed over the lake. Sam moved to stand next to him at the helm.

"This is freedom," she said.

Before he could second guess himself, Logan wrapped an arm around her waist and pulled Sam close. She smiled down at him, seemingly unconcerned about his lack of height. And why should she be? Once her stalker was caught, Sam would go back to her life.

Logan glanced over his shoulder to see Lauren letting her fingers skim the water. Both women were so down to earth it was hard to believe. Sam's face appeared in magazines, billboards, and on celebrity websites. Lauren was engaged to one of the wealthiest men in New York State. Yet they seemed content to glide along Lake Skaneateles in his tiny boat.

Sam's voice brought him back to the present. "Did you bring your binoculars?"

"Of course." Logan dropped his arm and reached under the helm.

Sam slung the strap around her neck and focused the lenses. "Check out that house," she said, pointing to a mansion hugging the shore.

"Hand me the binocs." Logan took the glasses and scanned the house. "This might be the house Justin Bieber bought." He handed the binoculars back.

"The Beebs?" Lauren asked. She craned her neck to look.

"See if you can get closer," Sam said, balancing the binoculars on her nose. "I think I see movement."

Logan was more interested in watching Sam than trying to get a glimpse of the famous celebrity. She looked cute, straining forward and scanning the shore in front of the mansion.

"See anything?" he asked.

Sam let the glasses drop. "No."

"A lot of rich and famous people are rumored to have vacation homes here."

"Like you?" Sam asked with a grin.

"Yeah. That's me. Rich and famous."

"Don't forget good looking."

Logan's face warmed. "And stylish, too. Thanks to my supermodel girl—I mean my friend."

He swung around to face the front of the boat, embarrassed he'd almost called Sam his girlfriend. What an idiot. The minute they got back to shore, she'd probably run for the hills. He didn't blame her. Why would she want to be associated with him, anyway? Aside from his money, he had nothing to offer.

Chapter 20

Sam wished their time on the lake could go on forever. Out here in this expanse of cerulean blue water she felt safe. Logan's arm around her both warmed and excited her. This man was different from the men she knew. Those few men she'd allowed closer had treated her like she couldn't be pretty *and* smart. They found ways to diminish her. For what purpose? Usually to make themselves feel better.

Or they paraded her around like a prize-winning purebred before trying to get her to compromise her morals. Although not super religious, her parents had taught her to respect herself and wait until marriage.

Logan's nerdy vibe comforted her. She couldn't see him trying to force himself on her. She hid a smile, thinking about how he'd almost called her his girlfriend. The truth was, she wouldn't have minded.

"Looks like we should head back." Logan used the rudder to turn the boat back toward his house.

"You're probably right," Sam said.

She watched Logan use the sails to tack back and forth, grabbing the last bit of wind to get them home. Home. Funny how this temporary rental was beginning to feel more like home than her apartment in the City.

When they passed the floating diving platform, Sam helped gather the sails and secure them. Logan started to motor and headed toward shore.

"What's that?" Lauren pointed to the deck of the rental.

A group of people clustered on Sam's back deck carrying cameras and microphones. In the space between her place and Logan's, she caught a glimpse of a news van. The side door stood open.

Sam's stomach clenched in panic. How had they found her?

"What's going on?" Lauren asked, getting up and standing next to her.

"Photographers." *Please don't let them see us.*

"Want me to motor back out?" Logan asked.

Sam shook her head. "Let's see if we can dock and slip into your house before they spot us."

By the time *Small Fry* bumped up against the deck, the crowd on her deck turned and noticed them tying up the craft.

"There she is!" someone shouted.

Like a flock of geese, they rushed to the stairs and shoved their way to the bottom. Logan helped her and Lauren step onto the dock.

"Go in the house," Logan said, his voice terse. He

strode to the edge of his property and held up his hands.

"This is private property. Leave now, or I'll call the police."

Sam heard the shouted questions as she and Lauren dashed for Logan's sliding door.

"Is it true you're in rehab?"

"Does Dawson know about your new boyfriend?"

"Why are you hiding?"

"Is that your new look?"

Safely inside, Sam stumbled to the sofa and dropped her head in her hands. "How did this happen?"

Lauren sank onto the sofa and wrapped her arms around Sam. "What are you going to do?"

Sam looked at her sister with tear-blurred eyes. "I don't know."

If paparazzi found her, how long until the stalker discovered her whereabouts?

It wasn't until Logan pulled out his phone to call the authorities that the group dispersed. But not before taking several photos of his frowning face. He'd managed to hold his responses to the questions hurled at him like grenades.

"Are you sleeping with Samantha?"

"Is she living with you?"

"What's your relationship?"

And finally, "What's your name?"

Logan watched until the last of the paparazzi pulled

away from the curb outside his house. How did she put up with such madness? He shuddered to think she dealt with that kind of attention regularly.

His phone dinged with a text.

Mandy: Ainsley's mom is bringing me home around eight.

With all the excitement, Logan had forgotten about his daughter. What kind of dad was he? The forgetful type. He'd enjoyed sailing with Sam and Lauren. And getting close to Sam. But that wasn't an excuse to forget his main responsibility.

Logan returned to his place and locked the door behind him. Lauren sat next to Sam on the couch, one arm around her shoulders and holding a box of tissues in the other.

"They're gone," he announced.

Sam looked up with tear-filled eyes. "Did you say anything to anybody about me being here?"

"Of course not." Her question stung. How could she think he'd alerted people to her whereabouts? "I told you your secret is safe with me."

"But how? It's probably my fault for going with you to the reunion thing. Maybe someone recognized me."

"Doubtful." But he'd figured it out. It was possible someone else had done the same.

Carmen appeared in the doorway to the living room. "I prepared some dinner."

Logan swiveled his head toward her. "Thanks,

Carmen. Go ahead and take it to the dining room."

"I don't think I can eat anything," Sam said, wiping her eyes.

"You need to eat," Lauren urged. She stood and held out a hand. Sam took it and let Lauren pull her to her feet.

Logan waited for the ladies to get seated before taking a seat. Carmen brought in a steaming dish of enchiladas and set it on the table. She returned a moment later with a wooden bowl filled to the brim with a salad.

"This looks great, Carmen. Thanks."

"Of course, Mr. Logan." Carmen beamed and scurried back to the kitchen.

Logan dished up the hot food on each of the women's plates and passed the salad bowl first to Sam and then to Lauren.

"While we eat, let's make a plan to keep you out of sight," Logan said.

"I should go back to New York and hide in my apartment," Sam said.

"That's the first place they'll look. Not a good idea."

"I agree," Lauren said. "They're probably camped out there now."

"I think you both should stay here."

Sam's fork clattered to her plate, breaking the silence that hung in the room for a moment.

"Are you serious?"

Logan set his fork down and leaned against the chair back. "It makes the most sense. I have plenty of room for you and your sister. No one knows who I am. I can keep the photographers away."

He glanced at Lauren to gauge her reaction. Her slow nod encouraged him to continue.

"Even if your stalker discovers the address of my rental, he won't know you've moved in here. He may think you've left the area completely."

"Hide in plain sight," Lauren said.

"Exactly."

Sam's head was bowed over her plate. Logan couldn't see her face. "Sam?"

She looked up with a deep sigh. "I guess."

"Good. Lauren and I will go over after dinner and get your things."

A ghost of a smile crossed Sam's face. "You sure are bossy."

"Only when dealing with recalcitrant supermodels."

Lauren chuckled. "I'm glad someone else is bossing her. She never listens to me."

Chapter 21

Logan followed Sam's sister to the rental and stepped through the back door into chaos.

"Did someone trespass and make this mess?" He gazed around the living room at the clothing draped over chairs, the sofa, and on the floor. Used dishes sat on the coffee table, along with empty to go cartons.

Lauren had begun to pick clothes up and drape them over her left arm. "My sister is a bit of a slob."

"That's an understatement," Logan muttered. He'd never been able to function surrounded by clutter. It might have been a mistake to ask Sam to stay with him. Carmen was diligent about keeping his home spotless. Even Mandy knew not to leave anything lying around. No sweater, hoodie, or electronic device could be within eyesight. *Why, yes, I am OCD.* It was one of the quirks of his diagnosis. It had driven Vivian mad. One of the many nails in the coffin of his marriage.

"Do you need some help?" Logan asked as Lauren bustled around the room.

"I've got this. You relax."

Logan descended the stairs in the basement and double-checked the hot water heater. Satisfied the pilot light was still lit, he wandered around the room, noting if anything required the attention of the property manager.

Satisfied that all was good, he climbed the stairs as Lauren appeared, dragging two suitcases.

"Need help?" he offered.

"That'd be great. I'll get our other bags."

"Let's go out the front," Logan suggested when they were loaded down with suitcases and travel bags. "We won't have to battle the deck stairs."

"Great idea."

They walked down the driveway to the street and turned left to go into Logan's drive. A white SUV pulled in as he and Lauren reached the front porch.

Mandy climbed out of the back. "What's going on?"

"Go in the house and I'll explain." Logan nodded to Tiffany, who'd rolled down her window.

"Yoohoo, Logan." Tiffany wiggled her fingers in a wave. "I fed the girls dinner at my house."

Logan nodded his thanks, dragging Sam's suitcase over the brick porch steps.

"Tell Sam I said hello!"

Before Logan could respond, Tiffany zipped up the window and rolled out of his driveway.

Mandy held the front door open while Lauren

entered the house.

"Again, Dad. What's going on?"

"Sam and Lauren are going to stay here for a while."

"Why?"

"It's complicated." Logan motioned for Lauren to take her bags up the stairs. He followed, Mandy on his heels.

"That's something you say to a child. I am not a child, Dad."

Logan's impatience came out when he answered. "Give me a moment, will you?"

Mandy froze. "Fine."

Logan sighed when she whirled around and clomped down the stairs. After he'd settled Lauren into one of the guest rooms and placed Sam's things in the other, he returned to the living room to find Sam and Mandy both scrolling through their phones.

Mandy spared him a glare before focusing again on her screen. "Sam won't say anything, and I want to know what's going on."

Logan glanced toward the stairs, but Lauren hadn't come down yet. Sam met his gaze but stayed quiet.

"Mandy, someone found out that Sam isn't who she says she is."

Mandy narrowed her eyes. "Okay. Who is she?" She turned toward Sam. "Who are you?"

Sam looked up with watery eyes. "It's all over social media."

Mandy huffed out a breath. "*What's* all over social media?"

"Mandy," Logan said, sitting next to her. "Sam is Samantha Jensen."

"Who?"

"The supermodel."

Mandy glanced from him to Sam. "I don't get it."

"There's a crazy guy stalking me," Sam said. "I had to change my appearance and hide out until he loses interest or is caught. Somehow, someone found out where I'm staying, and a bunch of photographers showed up next door."

"Lauren and Sam will be staying here until it's safe."

Sam snapped her fingers. "I'll be it was Frank. The staff photographer. Remember he came the other day to drop off my mail?"

"Makes sense," Logan said. "But why would he jeopardize his job by doing that?"

Sam snorted. "Money."

Mandy's face turned white. "I … I think I did something bad."

"What is it, Mandy?" Logan asked. Alarm bells sounded in his head.

Mandy licked her lips. "When we left the community center, Ainsley's mom said she knew someone who went to Hornell High. That's where Lauren said she graduated from. I guess she did a little digging and found your sister's picture in the yearbook."

"And maybe found mine too. I knew I should have stayed home."

Mandy met Logan's eyes. "There's more. I'm so sorry." Tears filled her eyes. "I had no idea."

"What are you talking about, Mandy?" Logan asked.

Mandy's tears dripped down her cheeks. "I took that picture of you guys in front of the backdrop." Her words sped up. "I posted it on X and Insta. I said Sam was your girlfriend."

Sam's mouth dropped open and snapped closed. "Are you kidding me right now?"

"I'm sorry, Sam. I really am. I didn't know …" Her voice trailed off as she sobbed.

Sam sprang to her feet. "This is all your fault," she said, pointing at Logan. She dashed up the stairs, and Logan heard a door slam.

"Dad?" Mandy said. "How can I fix this?"

Logan slumped back against the sofa cushion. "I don't know. What were you thinking?"

Mandy took several moments to answer. Her voice was soft. "My friends at school always tease me about you."

"Your friends." What kind of friends did his daughter have?

"I know it's wrong to let them bother me. But they make fun of you because you're weird. I thought if I showed them you have a girlfriend, they'd stop."

Logan remembered far too well what it was like to be bullied. Whether it was because of his clothes or his dad or because he was smart, it didn't matter. Kids were vicious. Cruel.

He scooted closer to his daughter and put an awkward arm around her shoulder. "What can we learn from this?"

"I don't know." Mandy sobbed again, her shoulders shaking.

"Why don't you go up to your room and think about it."

When she'd gone upstairs, Logan stepped out onto the deck, enveloped by the cool embrace of the evening. Darkness had descended like a velvet curtain, casting a serene hush over the tranquil lake. The lights from a scattering of homes along the shoreline flickered gently, sending a warm, welcoming glow that danced upon the water's surface. The soft, rhythmic lap-lap of the water against the shore created a soothing symphony.

Logan strolled to the end of his pier, the wooden boards creaking softly underfoot, and stood with his hands tucked into his pockets. The cool breeze ruffled his hair as he gazed out over the vast expanse of water. What had he gotten himself into? The question lingered in his mind, as vast and deep as the lake before him.

Sam sat with her back against the headboard, arms

wrapped around her knees. Lauren sprawled on the end of the bed.

"Skyler is blowing up my phone," Sam said as the device buzzed yet again.

"Maybe you should call her," Lauren suggested.

"I'm not quite ready to get an earful from her."

"Has she said anything about your stalker?"

"No. And I'm seriously considering going back to the City. I'm tired of hiding out. Tired of looking like a freak."

"What about Logan?" Lauren pretended nonchalance, examining her nails.

"What about him?" At this moment, Sam was ready to see the last of Logan and his daughter.

"I thought you liked him."

She did. Maybe too much. What if it was merely a summer crush that would dissolve once she went back to her life? These past few days had been relaxing. More relaxing than any vacation to the exotic places she'd been to. Being on Logan's sailboat with the wind on her face was a simple pleasure she'd come to crave. And didn't realize how much she enjoyed.

Mandy had hinted her dad was super rich, but Logan's attitude toward it was so low key he almost seemed embarrassed. Lauren's fiancé, Paul, had no problem keeping a jet on standby and using a driver-slash-assistant to handle his business. The only evidence of Logan's money was his house, the house next door, and his full-time cook and housekeeper,

Carmen. Well, and his fancy car.

"I do like him," Sam said. "But what happens when I go back to work in the City?"

"Doesn't he have a place there too?"

"Yes, but—"

"And won't he be going back to the City when Mandy goes back to school?"

"Yes, but—"

"And does he feel the same? Does he like you enough to put up with you?"

Sam grabbed a pillow and chucked it in Lauren's direction. "Hey. You're supposed to be on my side."

Lauren grinned. "Can I help it if I want everyone to be as blissfully happy as me and Paul?"

"I'm not sure that's possible, Sis."

Lauren's phone rang with the unmistakable ring tone of their mother. The theme from the movie *Jaws*.

"Hi, Mom." Lauren put the phone on speaker.

"Why am I always the last to hear about what's going on with you and your sister? Sam is not answering her phone, and I'm going crazy here. Did you know reporters have been on my doorstep for the past hour?"

Sam covered her mouth to keep from laughing. Mom was such a drama queen.

"I'm sorry to hear that, Mom," Lauren said. "Sam's right here."

Sam sent her sister the stink eye.

"Sam? You're there? Why didn't you tell me you

were hiding out? Are you sick?" Mom gasped. "Are you *pregnant*?"

"I am neither sick nor pregnant. I'm in hiding because I have a stalker."

"Stalker? Where are the police on this? Are you under witness protection?"

"I'm staying with a friend. Lauren too."

"I'm worried sick, Samantha."

Sam felt a shaft of sympathy for their mother. She was annoying, critical, and judgmental, but she did love her and Lauren.

"Why are reporters on my front lawn?" Mom asked.

"Someone posted a photo of me on the internet."

"Who did that? I thought you were hiding. If you're hiding, how did someone take your picture?"

How to explain to their mother she'd let a teenage girl snap her photo.

Unless …

Frank had also taken her picture when he'd brought the mail. What if it was him and not Mandy? Frank had always been odd. Sam assumed he had autism. Oddness aside, he was a fabulous photographer with an eye for making her look good. What if Frank decided he wanted to earn a little extra cash. Or a lot, depending on who was paying.

Sam stood and retrieved her iPad from her travel bag. She did a quick search and found the 'breaking news' that she'd been discovered hiding out in Skaneateles.

"Mom, we'll call you back. Something just came up." Sam snatched the phone and disconnected.

"What was that about?" Lauren asked.

"Look." Sam turned the iPad to face Lauren. "Come and see this."

Lauren clambered up the bed and settled herself next to Sam. Sam scrolled through the photos with rising alarm. Picture after picture appeared.

She and Logan, standing close together on *Small Fry*.

Sam reclining on the chaise on the deck next door.

Grinning as she beat Logan at Cribbage.

"This is creepy," Lauren whispered.

"Someone has been spying on me using a telephoto lens." Chills swept through her, raising goosebumps on her arms and legs. Being in the camera's eye was one thing. Being spied on was terrifying.

Chapter 22

Logan gave up the pretense of trying to sleep. His watch face glowed with the time. One thirty. He threw back the covers and slid out of bed. He pulled a T-shirt over his head and patted it down over his stomach.

He padded down the stairs and into the kitchen.

"Might as well brew some coffee," he said, turning on the lights. The stainless-steel Jura Capresso machine gleamed under the LED light strip.

While the machine burbled through its cycle, Logan rested his hands on the counter and let his head drop between his arms.

"Is that for me?"

Logan jumped and whirled around to see Sam standing in the doorway. She wore a pair of pajama pants adorned with bright red hearts and an over-sized black T-shirt. 'Pajamas all day' was written on the front in pink cursive.

"I can make you one." Logan pulled his gaze away.

Even with her hair mussed and face drawn from stress, Sam made his pulse speed up and his mouth go dry.

"Give me that one and make one for you," Sam said, holding out a hand for the finished cup.

Logan shook his head and did what she asked. "Fine. But only this time."

"Mmm, this is good. I couldn't sleep. I'm guessing you have the same problem?"

Logan pushed the buttons to start the machine for another cup of brew. "Yes."

Sam set the cup down and used her hands to pull herself up onto the counter. Logan felt her eyes on his back. His hand shook as he reached for the cup and a few drops spilled onto the counter. He pulled a paper towel off the roll, mopped up the spill, and turned to face her.

"I'm really sorry about Mandy posting that picture." He leaned back against the counter and crossed his ankles.

Sam eyed him over the rim of her cup. "It wasn't her fault."

"Sure it was. She admitted to posting our picture on Instagram, X, and probably Snapchat."

Sam took another sip without answering.

"I sent her to her room," Logan continued. "She wanted to impress her friends that her dad had a girlfriend." Why was he telling Sam this? It was as if his mouth and his brain conspired together to humiliate him. "Her friends tease her because I'm weird." Logan kept his eyes focused on his bare feet.

His head shot up when Sam snorted.

"She isn't the only one in the history of the world to be teased about something that isn't her fault," Sam said. "When I was six feet tall at fourteen, I got called giraffe, sticks, bamboo legs, long-legged snipe, and much worse. My sister was called marshmallow, fluffy pillow, and fatso." She shrugged. "Kids are notoriously mean at that age."

"Yes, but that doesn't excuse her—"

"It wasn't her."

"What do you mean?"

"The pictures out there, the ones that brought all the paparazzi to the door, were taken with a high-power camera. Let me run up and get my iPad." She jumped off the counter and set her empty cup down.

Logan rinsed her cup and put it in the dishwasher while he waited for Sam to return. A sudden chill hit him that someone had spied on her. And possibly him.

How was that any different from him using his binoculars to try to get a glimpse of Derek Jeter or one of the former presidents?

Who's the crazy stalker now?

Sam stared at her reflection in the full-length mirror in the bedroom. She used her hands to finger-comb the mop of uneven hair. Before she could second-guess herself, she strode into the bathroom and swiped a bit of pink gloss across her lips.

She ran lightly down the stairs and into the kitchen. Logan stood in the same position, but she noticed her cup was missing. Shaking her head, she brought up the website for the latest celebrity gossip.

"Here, take a look at these."

Logan took the iPad from her and swiped quickly through the photos, then again more slowly. "This is alarming." Especially alarming was the one of him with his arm around Sam in his sailboat. "How did they get these?"

"I have no idea. I should probably call my manager. Skyler sent me a dozen texts and two voice mails. I didn't have the energy to deal with her last night."

She took the iPad back from him and set it on the counter. Wrapping her arms around herself, she said, "Thanks for letting me and Lauren stay here. I'm sorry you're dragged into this."

Logan pushed himself away from the counter. Taking a step closer, he reached out and brushed a strand of hair behind her ear. His touch was gentle and raised goosebumps on her arms. The good kind, not the ones like when she'd first seen the photos.

"I'm glad I'm here," Logan said softly. "I'll protect you."

Sam knew he would. That's the kind of man he was. Not some skinny boy in a man's body, more concerned with his looks than in taking care of a woman."

"Sam," Logan began, his voice barely above a

whisper but filled with raw emotion. "I ... I need to tell you something."

Sam turned to look at him, her eyes searching his face for any hint of what was to come. In that moment, everything seemed to stand still, as if the universe itself was holding its breath.

"Ever since we met, I've felt a connection with you unlike anything I've ever experienced," Logan confessed, his voice trembling slightly. "You're not just someone I need to protect. You're ... You're someone I care deeply about. But—"

Sam placed two fingers over his mouth. "Sh." She let her fingers drop and tilted her head down to kiss him. He froze, then pulled her close. His arms wrapped around her and pressed her body to his, deepening the kiss.

Whatever Logan was going to say was forgotten as they communicated without words. Logan was the first to pull away.

"We should stop before I'm tempted to carry you upstairs."

Sam let out a breath and let her head drop. Logan was right. They'd started a fire that could quickly blaze out of control.

"I'm going to head upstairs and try to get some sleep." Sam pushed away from the counter and took one last look into Logan's green eyes before pulling herself away.

When she reached the bedroom, Sam crawled back

into bed, curled on her side, and tried to sleep. Something tickled at the edge of her brain. The photos. Something about the pictures. Or was it something else?

Think about something else. Like kissing Logan. And his confession that he cared for her.

Sam fell into a troubled sleep and woke with a start. The sun peeked its way around the edges of the plantation shutters. She remembered what had eluded her last night. Frank had brought a manila envelope yesterday containing her mail. Lauren must have forgotten to grab it when she packed their things.

Sam slipped on a pair of flip flops and grabbed the keys to the rental. She tiptoed down the stairs and out the back door of Logan's house. The air was already thick with humidity.

Dew covered the grassy berm between the two houses, wetting her feet. Sam stumbled on the damp wood steps and crossed the deck.

The rental was neat, thanks to Lauren. She'd picked up all the discarded clothes and take out containers. Sam found the envelope Frank had given her in the kitchen. She grabbed it and hurried back to Logan's house.

She found Carmen in the kitchen, brewing a pot of coffee.

"You're up early, Miss Sam."

Sam smiled. "Yes, and I'll probably need a nap later. Can you bring me a cup of that when it's done?"

She pointed to the coffee maker.

"Of course."

"I'll be in the living room." Sam returned to the living room and sank onto the couch. She ripped open the envelope and let the contents spill onto the cushion next to her.

Bill, bill, request for money, and two nondescript white envelopes with no return address.

Sam's pulse sped up and her breath caught.

Chapter 23

Logan spent the rest of the night berating himself for his actions. He was like a love-sick teenager. He'd practically confessed undying love for Sam without waiting to see if she felt the same.

I'm so stupid.

Sam deserved someone a lot more … polished than he was. Someone she could be proud to have on her arm at the red-carpet events she attended.

But she had kissed him first.

As he rolled over for the umpteenth time, Logan remembered Sam had said her birthday was July 4. What if he planned a celebration? Something she'd never forget. She'd casually mentioned she hadn't had a real birthday party ever. 'Too busy working,' she'd said.

Time to fix that. He'd enlist Lauren's help.

He found Carmen in the kitchen holding a spatula in one hand and a steaming cup of coffee in the other.

"Brewed coffee?" he asked.

"You know I don't know how to use that fancy machine," Carmen said. "Your friend didn't complain."

"Friend?"

"Miss Sam. She is in the living room." Carmen handed him the mug. "Take this."

Logan carried his mug of coffee and found Sam hunched over what looked like a letter. She looked up when he entered. Her face was deathly pale.

Alarmed, Logan sat next to her. "What is it?"

Sam thrust a white sheet of paper toward him without speaking. Her hand shook. Logan pushed his glasses up his nose and read the words crudely printed there.

My dearest Samantha - I won't call you Sam because that is a man's name. You are my beautiful and lovely Samantha. I can hardly wait to make you mine. Soon my darling.

Panic made its way up from Logan's stomach and squeezed his chest. "This is terrible."

"There's more." Sam handed him another sheet of paper.

Logan read the words with growing alarm.

See you soon my darling.

"Have you alerted the authorities?" Logan asked. He read and reread the two letters.

"Not yet. I've barely had a chance to absorb them."

The chrome clock on the fireplace mantel chimed eight times.

"Let's wait an hour and call the police."

Sam reached for her phone on the coffee table. "I need to call my manager."

"Will she be up this early?"

"Probably not." Sam let the phone drop back into her lap. "I'm scared."

Logan was scared too. This crazy person could show up at any time. What was his end goal? To whisk Sam away to some lair and claim her as his possession?

"You should probably get away for a while. Maybe leave the country."

Sam's spine stiffened. "I'm tired of hiding. I refuse to be held captive any longer by fear."

"But—"

"I'm going back to New York City. Back to my apartment. Back to my career."

Logan wanted to say, what about us? But with a sinking sensation, he realized there was no 'us.' He was merely a diversion, a bump in the summer road that led her into his life.

"Let's wait and see what your manager says." Maybe she would talk some sense into her.

"Fine. But I'm going to insist."

"Insist what?" Lauren stopped in the doorway to the living room and rubbed her eyes.

"Let me get you some coffee," Logan said, standing and heading to the kitchen. Maybe Lauren could convince Sam to stay out of sight. At least until after her birthday.

Sam watched Lauren make her way to the opposite sofa. She looked rested, unlike what Sam had seen in her own reflection earlier. Dark circles stood out like bruises under her eyes. Her skin looked dry and lifeless, as did her hair.

"I went over to the rental this morning and found these." Sam thrust the scary letters in Lauren's direction.

"What were you thinking, going over by yourself?"

"I couldn't sleep. I remembered Frank had brought my mail, and I wanted to see if I needed to—"

"Sam, you can't do that again. What if this person finds you and …" Lauren's voice trailed off as she glanced down at the papers Sam handed her. "Oh, my gosh," Lauren whispered.

"Logan thinks I should leave the country."

"Good idea," Lauren said. "This is escalating. You need to call the police."

"I will. As soon as I call Skyler."

She'd call Skyler, the police, and after, she'd arrange for a car to pick her up and take her back to the City. There was no way she'd be able to stay here with Logan. Not with her growing feelings for him. She was falling for him. Hard. And it scared her almost as much as the stalker.

Chapter 24

Logan and Lauren huddled in the kitchen while Sam paced the living room, phone to her ear.

"Do you think Skyler can convince her to stay out of sight?" Logan asked.

"I hope so. I'm worried. Sam is convinced she can go back to normal and ignore these threats."

"I have an idea," Logan said, forming the plan as he spoke. "Sam's birthday is in two days. What if I take her someplace far away, just for a day or two, and give the authorities time to see if they can hone in on their search?"

"Where would you go?" Lauren asked.

"I'm not sure. Paris?"

Lauren sent him a skeptical look. "How will you convince Sam to go?"

"That's where you come in. We tell her I'm taking her on a date and … well, I haven't thought the rest of it through yet."

"I can help. I'll pack her bags, and you can sneak

them out of the house."

"Perfect. I'll make some arrangements, and we'll touch base later today."

Logan bounded up the stairs with his laptop under his arm. He hated working in his bedroom, but today he'd make an exception. First up, contact his virtual assistant and enlist her help. He sent an email outlining his needs.

Transportation to the local airport.

Contract private jet for transatlantic flight

Hotel in Paris

Pack clothes

Logan wracked his brain for any details he might have left out. His VA should be able to handle anything he'd forgotten. Except one thing. He needed to buy a birthday gift for Sam. What would be appropriate? Jewelry. Always a good choice.

But that would mean a trip into town. Logan's pulse pounded drum-like in his head. He pictured several scenarios where he'd be forced to interact with someone more knowledgeable about fine jewelry than he was. They'd probably snicker about his lack of refinement. It would be easier to order something online.

But for Sam, he'd brave the strangers' judgment and go to an actual brick and mortar store.

After a quick shower and even quicker shave, Logan returned downstairs to find Lauren and Sam with their heads bent over the remains of breakfast. Carmen appeared a moment later with another plate of bacon, eggs, and fried potatoes.

"Looks like you ladies already ate," Logan said.

Sam handed her empty plate to Carmen. "Thank you, Carmen. That was good."

"I'm glad to see you're eating, Miss Sam," Carmen said with a smile.

Logan was glad too. Sam needed her strength. This situation had to be harrowing for her. "Did you speak with your manager?"

"Skyler is going to handle the police," Sam said. "I sent her a screen shot of the letters, and she said she'd pass them on."

"What did she say about you returning to work?" Logan held his breath waiting for her answer.

Sam's mouth turned down. "She won't let me come back. She'd already rearranged my schedule, so I have no work planned until after the first of August."

Logan forced his face to stay neutral, but he wanted to jump up and down. His plan would work perfectly. "So, you'll stay here until then?"

"Probably not. I can't take advantage of your hospitality that long."

"It's no bother," Logan said. "I have plenty of room. And Mandy would love to have you stay."

Sam exchanged a look with her sister. "Lauren is going back to Keuka Lake tomorrow. Won't it be awkward having me here?"

"Not at all." What did she mean by awkward?

"Let me think about it," Sam said, pushing her chair back. "I'm going to take a shower."

After Sam left, Logan dug into his breakfast. Carmen was a lifesaver. He'd never be able to cook for himself, much less Mandy. Too bad Carmen wouldn't or couldn't go with him when summer was over, and he returned to the City.

Lauren leaned over and whispered, "Did you come up with a plan?"

"My VA is working on it. I hope to leave tonight. Do you think you can distract Sam long enough to get her stuff packed?"

"I don't think she's unpacked since we moved in yesterday. Why don't you take her out on your sailboat later? I can get everything loaded into your car while you're gone."

"Actually, I'm having a car service come and take us to the airport."

"Perfect." Lauren beamed at him, and Logan grinned back. He felt like a kid planning a surprise for his mom.

Before she left him and his dad, his mom had been his everything. She'd defended him against Dad's criticism of his 'softness.' Logan had preferred quiet activities like reading or making things with his hands. Dad had wanted a more study boy. One who'd share his interest in all things sports.

When that didn't happen, Dad turned to heaping him with shame. After all this time, Logan still felt the sting of his dad's disappointment. Even though Logan had set his dad up in a paid-off house in the nearby town of Auburn, Dad still threw barbs on the few times per year Logan visited him.

Logan shook off the memories and hoped Sam would enjoy the surprise he had planned.

"Ready to go?"

Sam glanced from Logan to her sister. "You two look guilty."

"Not at all," Lauren said. "Enjoy the lake."

Sam narrowed her eyes. Was her sister conspiring with Logan to plan something for her upcoming birthday? She should never have mentioned to Logan she'd not had a proper birthday party. If she came back after sailing to a surprise party, she'd never forgive Lauren.

On the other hand, who could Lauren invite? Sam was supposed to be hiding.

"What about the reunion committee?" Sam asked, stalling.

"Taken care of," Logan said. "I told Tiffany we were busy today."

"What about Mandy and lacrosse practice."

"No practice today," Logan said. "Stop stalling ,and let's get out onto the lake before the wind dies down."

"Fine." Sam hmphed and grabbed a towel from Logan's hands.

They clomped down the pier and into *Small Fry*. It wasn't that Sam didn't want to go sailing. But she was terrified of being alone with Logan again. She might not be able to keep from grabbing him and kissing him senseless.

Where was her normally cool personality? Logan had swept it away like the wind now carrying them down the center of Lake Skaneateles. The small boat glided over the water like a swan. Logan stood with one hand on the mast and one hand shielding his eyes from the sun. Sam admired the way he seemed so comfortable in his sailboat, wearing a tattered T-shirt and one of his new pair of shorts. He had nice legs, well-shaped and not too hairy. He'd shoved his feet into a pair of navy blue Hey Dudes. At least he wasn't wearing socks this time.

She turned her gaze to the shoreline before Logan could catch her staring. Was she attracted to him simply because he was different than the men she normally came in contact with? Or was it because he represented something Sam craved—normalcy. These past several days had shown her there was life outside of modeling. She'd been able to let down and go without makeup and perfectly chosen clothes. It had been a relief to just be. To help paint a backdrop for Logan's class reunion. To play Cribbage with Mandy. To kiss someone without having to shove him away when he tried to go further.

Was this what she wanted? A normal life, away from the spotlight? Away from having to perform all the time? Was she what Logan wanted? To quote the famous *Notting Hill* line, did he want 'a girl, standing in front of a boy, asking him to love her?'

Did she love Logan? Or did she love his life?

Logan tied off the sail and sat beside her in the stern. "You look serious. What are you thinking about?"

Sam sucked in a breath and let it out in a whoosh. "What are we doing, Logan?"

"We're sailing."

"I don't mean this. I mean, us. Is there an 'us?' We are so different. I'm a slob, and you're obsessively clean. I perform in front of a camera, and you get a panic attack when you have to go out in public. You're—"

Before she could finish, Logan turned and pulled her to him, cutting off her words with his lips on hers. When she could no longer breathe, he released her and sat back.

"What was that?" Sam said.

"That is what we're doing. If there isn't an 'us,' there should be. Sam, I—"

"Hey, watch where you're going!" The shout brought Logan to a stand. He grabbed the rudder and turned it in time to avoid a party barge full of college-age men and women.

"Sorry!" Logan said. Several of the revelers made lewd comments about catching them kiss. Some of the girls threw them air kisses followed by shrieks of laughter.

Logan consulted his watch and turned *Small Fry* back toward his house.

"Guess we're done sailing," Sam muttered. What had Logan been about to say?

Chapter 25

Logan checked his email on his phone and smiled. His VA had come through. Everything was in place for an impromptu trip to Paris. Nerves skittered up his spine. He'd never done anything so rash and irrational ever. This could either be the most romantic thing ever or a colossal disaster.

He would know by tomorrow.

Logan guided his boat into the slip next to his dock and tied the ropes onto the cleats. He held a hand out to help Sam clamber onto the wood planks.

"Thank you," she said, releasing his hand. "We still need to finish our conversation."

"Let's go inside and get something to drink. We can talk in the car."

"Car? Where are we going?"

"Just a short ride. You'll see."

"Fun fact about Samantha," she said. "I don't like surprises."

Logan's stomach tumbled. Was it too late to back

out of his well-crafted plan?

Mandy greeted them from the sliding glass door. "Dad, Ainsley wants to know if I can go with them to the City. Her mom wants to go shopping. Can I go?"

"Will Ainsley's brother be going too?" Logan sincerely hoped not. He wasn't ready for his daughter to have a crush on an older boy. He might never be ready.

"Daxton is staying home with his dad. Please can I go?"

"When will you be back?" This might work out perfectly. He wouldn't have to ask Carmen to watch Mandy.

"We're leaving in an hour, and we'll be gone two nights. We're staying at Ainsley's mom's and dad's apartment in the City. Please say yes." Mandy implored him with puppy-dog eyes.

"Fine. But be aware of your surroundings. Stay with Ainsley's mom. Don't go out by yourselves."

Mandy rolled her eyes. "I know, I know. Can I have your debit card?"

Logan heard Sam stifle a laugh behind him. "My wallet is on my dresser."

Mandy bounced up and down on her toes. "Thanks, Dad. What's my limit?"

Logan had to think. What was an appropriate amount? "Uh, no more than a thousand."

Mandy's mouth dropped open. "Okay." She whirled and dashed up the stairs.

"Was that too much?" Logan asked, turning to Sam.

She shrugged. "I have no idea. I guess if you have the money, you can do whatever."

Logan second-guessed his decision. How could he ever get the hang of this parenting thing when the rules were not defined.

He froze in indecision while Sam headed into the kitchen. She returned a few minutes later with two bottles of water. She thrust one in his direction.

"Drink this. You look parched."

"More like gobsmacked, to use an appropriate British term. I have no idea what I'm doing."

"I'll bet every parent feels the same. Don't worry, Mandy won't spend that much. She's a good kid, Logan."

"No thanks to me." He rolled the bottle across his burning hot forehead.

Footsteps sounded on the tile entry floor. Lauren peeked her head into the living room. "I'm all packed. I'm heading back to Paul's place now."

Sam walked to her and pulled her into a hug. "I'm going to miss you, Sis."

"I'll miss you too. But you're in good hands." Lauren sent Logan a wink over Sam's shoulder.

A horn beeped twice outside the front door.

"That's the car I ordered," Logan said. "We'll go with you."

Sam sent him a questioning look. "All the way to Lake Keuka?"

"Not that far. You girls go ahead and get in the car.

I'm going to say goodbye to Mandy."

Logan dashed upstairs and found Mandy throwing clothes into a Foldie bag.

"Mandy, I'm going to be gone for a couple of days, too. If you need me, text, okay?"

Mandy glanced up and pushed the hair away from her face. "Where are you going?"

Logan felt his face grow warm. "Paris."

Mandy's hands dropped to her side. "Paris?"

"For Sam's birthday."

Mandy held his gaze for several seconds. "You really like her, don't you?"

Logan slowly nodded, uncomfortable having this conversation with this fourteen-year-old daughter.

"Do you love her?"

Logan nodded again. He did love Sam. How was that possible after only a little over a week?

"You better go, Dad," Mandy said. She grinned at him and reached out to hug him. Soon she'd be taller than he was. He'd have to get used to being surrounded by tall women.

If Sam felt the same way.

A double tap on the horn outside motivated him to kiss Mandy on the top of her head and dash back down the stairs.

"You look like the cat who swallowed the cream," Sam said as she and Lauren waited inside the Lincoln

Town Car.

"I have no idea what you're talking about," Lauren said with a sniff.

"Hm. You're a terrible liar." Sam leaned forward to speak to the dark-suited driver. "Where are we going?"

He kept his gaze forward and didn't answer. Sam sat back and crossed her arms. "I hate surprises," she grumbled.

"I think you won't mind this one," Lauren said.

Logan pulled open the front passenger door and climbed in. He nodded to the driver, who put the car in motion. Logan turned around and said, "We're going to the airport to see a man about a plane."

"That doesn't sound cryptic at all," Sam said. Logan turned back around without answering.

Soon the driver pulled the vehicle into Syracuse International Airport. Sam read the signs as they passed by the commercial flight area and into the private plane service lot. The car stopped in front of a series of steel buildings.

"Here you go, sir," the driver said. He exited the car and went to the back, opening the trunk.

"Ready?" asked Logan.

"Ready for what?" Why was the driver wheeling her suitcase and carryon toward a sleek-looking jet sitting on the tarmac?

"Just say yes," Lauren said, leaning over to give Sam a quick hug.

Logan opened the passenger door and held out his

hand. Sam let herself be pulled from the car. "What's going on?" she asked. She glanced from her sister, grinning from the inside of the car, and Logan, standing stiffly with his arms at his sides.

"We're going to see a man about a plane," Logan repeated. "Let's go." He took her hand and tugged her in the direction of the plane.

Sam allowed herself to be led across the hot asphalt and up the steps into the waiting jet. The interior was blessedly cool. A unformed flight attendant flashed a smile at her as she moved aside to allow Sam to enter.

"Welcome. Please sit anywhere."

Sam turned to Logan. "Are we sitting or flying or . . ."

Logan pointed toward two seats. "Aisle or window?"

Sam shrugged. "It doesn't matter."

"You take the window, and I'll sit in the aisle seat."

The flight attendant appeared a moment later with two champagne glasses. "Enjoy a mimosa while we do our final checks."

Sam held the glass in one hand and grabbed Logan's arm with the other. "Where are we going?" she hissed.

"You'll see."

Tempted to down the entire mimosa in one gulp, Sam took a sip and considered getting up and running for the door. But the flight attendant was already pulling in the steps and securing the door.

"Relax," Logan said. "I promise you'll enjoy this."

Sam glared at him. "I better or else you'll never hear the end of it."

Logan smiled. "Did you know a Cessna Citation Longitude has a maximum cruise speed of four hundred eighty-three knots? That's roughly eight hundred ninety kilometers per hour." He glanced at his watch. "You might want to relax. Lean back, grab a pillow."

"What? Why?" Sam's pulse sped up.

The flight attendant appeared to take their champagne glasses. "We'll be taking off in less than five minutes. I'll get you comfortable after we're in the air."

"Where are we going?" Sam asked.

"Paris."

Before Sam could respond, the woman strode to the back of the plane.

"Paris?" Sam said, renewing her glare in Logan's direction. But he had his eyes closed and his face wore a slight smile. Sam jabbed him in the ribs with an elbow. "Are you kidnapping me?"

Logan opened one eye. "Happy birthday, Sam."

Chapter 26

After this flight, Sam was never going to speak to Logan again. How dare he whisk her on a private jet and take her across the Atlantic to a foreign country. The nerve! And to Paris!

She'd been to Paris several times, always on a strict schedule of photo shoots. She'd never had more than a few hours to explore the most romantic city in the world.

Sam woke to the bump of the plane hitting the runway. Logan was no longer seated beside her. He was across the aisle, reading a paperback book. Sam took a moment to admire his profile. His full head of brown hair curled over his collar in the back. A dark stubble covered his cheek. She imagined what it would be like to wake up to that face every day.

You're getting ahead of yourself, girlfriend. They hadn't had the 'define the relationship' talk. Each time, they'd been interrupted. And Sam was still slightly miffed that she'd been picked up and spirited away without being asked. She needed to give Lauren a piece of her mind too for being complicit in the deception.

Sam peered out the window. Dawn was breaking over the magical city. Sam's pulse sped up. A whole day to spend in Paris with no agenda. She couldn't wait to get started.

The flight attendant strode up the middle aisle carrying a tray with two steaming towels. "Here you go," she said. "I'll be back in a moment with coffee."

Sam used the towel to refresh her face and neck, breathing in the eucalyptus scent. "Mm. Wonderful." She sent a smile in Logan's direction, noticing he looked relieved at her mood.

The coffee was perfect, too. Hot, black, and strong. "A girl could get used to this," she said.

"I thought with your lifestyle, you'd already be used to this."

Sam shook her head. "I mostly fly commercial. This is amazing." She waved a hand around the cabin.

"Maybe I should invest on one of these. Instead of *Small Fry*, I could name it *Big Fry*."

Sam laughed at his feeble attempt at humor. "How about *Super-Size*?"

"Ah. Even better."

Sam's excitement grew as they deplaned and headed for a waiting car. "Where to?" she asked.

"I thought we could head to the hotel first. Get cleaned up. Then have breakfast. What do you think?"

"Perfect. But will we be able to check in to the hotel

this early?"

"I'm sure we can."

Sam craned her neck to peer at the passing scenery as they left the airport and drove into the city. Such a different landscape than New York. She marveled at the ancient buildings, so full of character and charm. They were soon inside the city on narrow roads more suited to the Smart Cars and Mini Coopers zipping past them. What fun to rent a couple of Vespas and simply ride around the City. Maybe she'd suggest it to Logan.

Unless he had other plans. What if he only rented one hotel room? Was this trip a way to trick her into sleeping with him? She'd heard nightmare stories from other female models about being taken advantage of. Dazzled with fancy meals, exotic trips, and expensive jewelry, onto so the guy could brag he'd bagged a supermodel.

But Logan wasn't like that. She hoped.

Logan sensed Sam's sudden mood change and chalked it up to exhaustion from the past few days of drama. He hoped she'd relax once they got checked into their hotel and had eaten breakfast.

Logan couldn't have been happier with this VA's attention to detail. She'd been practically giddy at being given *carte blanche* to create a memorable trip, short as it was.

They arrived at the Ritz Carlton and the driver

jumped out to open the back door so they could climb out. A doorman appeared and took their bags from the trunk.

Logan tipped the driver and the doorman and put a hand on the small of Sam's back as they entered the lobby. No one raised an eyebrow, though they were dressed more for a backyard barbecue than for a trip to a metropolitan city.

Sam stood with her hands clasped together while Logan registered and retrieved their keys. "We have adjoining suites," Logan told her, watching Sam's shoulders sag. Relief?

Another employee took their bags on a rolling cart and led them to the elevators. "Floor?" he asked.

"Six," Logan said. They remained silent while the elevator ascended to their floor.

"Here you go, Sir." He held his hand out for the key to Sam's room. He opened the door with a flourish. "This is our Deluxe Suite," the man said.

Sam followed him into the room and slowly turned in a circle.

"Will this work?" Logan asked.

"It'll do," Sam replied. Her face held a small smile.

"How long do you need to get ready?"

"Give me an hour to shower and change. I'm starved."

"Sounds good."

Logan followed the employee down the hall to another suite. Once the man had closed the door behind him, Logan sent a text to Mandy.

Logan: Everything good there?

He didn't expect an answer, calculating the six-hour time difference in his head. It would be past midnight in New York If Mandy did, indeed, respond, he'd have to chastise her for being up so late.

He showered, shaved, and changed into a pair of dark slacks and a white button-up shirt. He pulled on a patterned sport coat against the morning chill. His watch showed he still had fifteen minutes before Sam said she'd be ready.

He sent a quick text to her.

Logan: I'll be in the lobby. No hurry.

He sat on a stiff chair in the hotel lobby and watched the early-morning comings and goings. A few people looked like they'd just returned from an evening of partying. Stumbling a little on the slick tile floor and laughing at their clumsiness.

Logan's attention was drawn to a commotion near the elevators. The doors had swished open, and several people tried to board at once, creating a minor bit of chaos. After shouts of good-natured laughter, Sam extricated herself from the group and strode toward him.

Logan's breath caught. She'd done something to her hair, something different. The crazy-cut ends were tamed into a sleek chin-length bob. Dark liner accentuated her blue eyes, and pink lipstick pulled his eyes to her mouth.

She stopped in front of him. "Do I look okay?" She ran a hand down her pale pink capris. She wore a flowered top with a soft pink sweater that grazed her waist.

Logan tried to swallow. "Uh, yes. Fine."

Sam's smile was smug, as if she knew exactly the impact she had on his out-of-control heartbeat. "Let's eat," she announced. "I'm starved."

Chapter 27

Sam insisted they visit every little clothing boutique along the street. She chatted easily with the shop owners in a mixture of her basic French and English. Logan watched in amusement as Sam charmed the women who willingly showed her their latest styles. It didn't hurt that Sam purchased something from each shop.

By the time they reached the Montmartre area, his arms were ready to fall out of their sockets.

"Let's stop and get something to drink," Logan said, spying yet another sidewalk cafe in the next block.

"Sure."

Sam seemed to thrive on the activity while he was ready to crawl back to the hotel and hibernate.

"This is fun," Sam said, dropping onto a metal chair at a tiny bistro table. "Thanks for being my pack mule."

"Your pack mule is about ready to call it quits," Logan said, setting the packages on an extra chair.

The waiter appeared, and Sam ordered sparkling

water for both of them. "Oh, and an espresso for my friend," Sam said, smiling up at the hovering waiter.

He nodded and disappeared into the dark interior of the bar. "You need a pick-me-up," Sam said. "We still have to check out the Montmartre."

Logan groaned. "When do you run out of gas?"

Sam's eyes sparkled as she leaned her arms on the table. "Never."

Logan groaned again. "May I plead for mercy?"

Sam sat back and eyed him. "I'll tell you what. After this, let's go back to the hotel, and you can take a nap, or whatever you old people do. I'll go out by myself. There are a couple of designers I want to see while we're here."

Alarm bells went off in Logan's head. "By yourself? I don't think so."

Sam sighed. "I'll be fine. You can hire a car for me. I'll be perfectly safe."

Logan didn't try to argue. His feet hurt and his head ached. He needed a quiet, dark hotel room to recharge. "Fine. But you'll come back if you see anything suspicious, okay?"

Sam's face clouded. "I doubt my stalker followed me here. But I promise to be careful."

They sat in silence, watching the crowd ebb and flow around them. Drinks finished, Logan flagged down a taxi to take them back to the Ritz.

"Want to grab a bite of lunch before you go back out?"

Sam shook her head. "I'm still full from breakfast. You go ahead, though."

"I think I'll get room service." While Sam went to the ladies' room, Logan went to the concierge and ordered a car service for the afternoon and evening.

"The car will be outside in ten minutes," he said when Sam came out of the restroom.

"Thanks." She leaned toward him and gave him a quick peck on the cheek. "Can you ask them to put the bags in my room?"

Logan nodded his assent and headed toward the elevator. He turned to watch Sam stride through the lobby. Men and women stopped their conversations to watch the tall woman breeze toward the door.

He was a lucky man. So far.

"This fabric is wonderful," Sam said, rubbing the sleeve of a pale blue jacket between her thumb and forefinger.

"I'm glad you appreciate it." The designer flushed with pleasure at Sam's compliment. "It isn't often we get someone of your stature in our humble studio."

Sam knew it had less to do with her 'stature' and more to do with her status. The designer had fallen all over himself to show Sam his latest creations. He hoped to break into the American market and might be able to with Sam's stamp of approval.

She turned to the obsequious young man. "You

know, if you let me take a sample or two back with me, I might be able to convince the right people to connect with you."

An hour later, Sam had made no specific promise, but she'd acquired the adorable jacket she'd admired and an evening dress to die for.

"Wait till Logan sees this," she said, doing a little jig on her way out of the shop to the waiting car.

She stopped at the hotel lobby desk and asked for room service to send up a bottle of sparkling water and a fruit basket to her room. That should tide her over until dinner.

In her room, Sam sent a text to Lauren.

Sam: Paris is amazing. I bought something for you. Love you!

She tossed the phone on the bed and fell back onto the soft coverlet. She hadn't had this much fun in forever. Most of her clothes were hand-picked by either Skyler, Manny, or one of the designers on staff. Everything she'd bought today, and the things Logan had paid for, were all of her own choosing. Too bad there were no photographers. What she planned to wear to dinner tonight would knock their socks off.

She'd have to be content to knock Logan's socks off. She smiled remembering his calf-length black socks and Velcro sneakers the first time she'd see him.

You've come a long way, baby. Speaking of Logan, her phone pinged with a text.

Logan: Dinner at 9.

She sent a thumbs up emoji, then draped the down comforter over her for another indulgence—a much-needed nap.

She woke to another text.

Logan: Meet me in the lobby at 8:30

Samantha took her time getting ready. She mentally thanked Lauren for packing her cosmetics, and she used them to darken her pale eyebrows and eyelashes. Adding some color to her cheeks and eyelids completed the look of casual yet elegant.

She shimmied into the dress she'd wrangled from the new designer and observed herself in the mirror. Except for her hair, she looked like her old self. The sheath dress was pale silver and swished around her knees. The tailored jacket worked perfect to create a stunning chic look. With a smile, she grabbed her handbag and headed out the door to meet Logan.

Chapter 28

How many times would Sam take his breath away? She exited the elevator and glanced his way with a smile. Her mile-long legs peeked out from below a gray dress. The suit-like jacket hugged her hips in the right places.

"Wow. You look amazing," Logan said as he stood to greet her.

"Thanks. You look pretty amazing, too."

Logan felt his cheeks warm. "I did a little shopping today too."

Sam looked him up and down. "Not bad."

Logan held out his arm and Sam hooked her arm through his. "Where are we going?" she asked.

"I can't remember." All thoughts fled from his brain from the pressure of Sam's arm. "I told the driver."

"I'm sure we will get there in one piece."

A car sat idling in front of the hotel. A uniformed man jumped out and opened the rear door with a flourish.

"*Merci*," Sam said as they climbed in.

Logan couldn't have spoken even if he wanted to. He was escorting one of the most beautiful women on this continent on a dinner date. What a difference from his life before Sam. Was it only a few weeks ago he was glued to his laptop and oblivious to the world?

While they rode to the restaurant, Sam chattered nonstop about her afternoon. Logan listened and responded appropriately at the proper time. But his attention was on the small jewelry box he'd tucked into his jacket pocket. Would Sam like what he picked out? Was it too intimate, too soon, for jewelry?

He was out of his league.

The car jerked to a stop. "We have arrived," the driver said in heavily accented English.

"Thank you." Logan waited for him to open the back door. He slid out and held out his hand for Sam's. It slipped easily into his and he held it as they walked across the sidewalk and into the restaurant.

Over his shoulder, he addressed the driver. "We will see you in a couple of hours."

The driver touched his hand to his cap and returned to the vehicle.

A doorman greeted them, opening the door wide and motioning them in. Sam spoke to the hostess in her combination of French and English, looking to Logan for confirmation that he'd made a reservation.

"But of course." The hostess led them to a table

near the window.

Logan couldn't help notice the stares from the men seated at tables with their wives, girlfriends, or business associates. They were probably wondering why such an ugly guy was with a beautiful woman like Sam. Even in her low-heeled sandals, she was at least a head taller than him.

Once they were seated, a waiter appeared at the table asking if they'd like something to drink. Logan glanced at Sam. She shrugged.

"White wine, please," Logan said. When he'd walked away, Logan said, "I don't drink much, but it seems appropriate to order wine when in France, don't you think?"

"I don't drink much, either. Too many calories." Sam made a face. "Once I get back to work, I'll have to focus more on my diet." She patted her still-flat stomach.

"This restaurant has a prix fixe menu. I ordered ahead. Hope that's okay." Logan held his breath while Sam seemed to consider his words

"Sounds good."

Their wine was poured, and Logan held his glass up. "Happy birthday," he said, clinking his glass with Sam's.

"I totally forgot. I'm not used to celebrating my birthday."

"Not even as a kid?"

Sam frowned. "My mom used to tell me all the

fireworks on July 4 were for me. She said the whole country celebrated my birthday. I was nine before I figured out the truth."

"I can't imagine what that must have been like."

"What about you? Any birthday stand out to you from your childhood?"

Logan took a sip of his wine and set the glass down. "Not really. My dad wasn't into celebrations."

"What about your mom?"

"She left when I was twelve. It was just my dad and me after that." Logan still felt the twin emotions of guilt and shame of his mom's leaving. Dad blamed him, saying if Logan wasn't so stupid and ugly, Mom wouldn't have left. Twenty four months of therapy, and he still struggled.

"That's terrible. I'm so sorry." Sam laid a hand on Logan's arm.

"Enough about me. Tell me about your childhood."

"Ugh. It was anything but normal. I was in and out of school from eighth grade through high school."

"I remember reading about that. You started modeling at fourteen. You were in two cereal commercials and a Pepsi commercial. You signed with Top Notch Talent when you turned eighteen. You've been featured in *Vogue*, *Elle*, and a host of other magazines."

Sam leaned back in her chair. "I don't know whether to be flattered or alarmed."

"The internet is a wonderful thing."

"Apparently. What else did you read?"

"You've been linked romantically with Dawson Knox, but I don't think there's anything there. Your body language in the photos indicate there are no feelings between you."

"Very astute. Dawson and I aren't even friends. We've never had a significant conversation about anything."

"Sounds awful."

The waiter appeared and set small plates of salad in front of them. He bowed without a word and disappeared again.

"Do you get along with your dad?" Sam asked.

Logan took a forkful of salad while he considered how to answer. "We get along as long as I don't see him. He lives about twenty minutes from my place on the lake."

"Why are our relationships with our parents so difficult?" Sam asked.

Sam let the flavors of the salad linger on her taste buds. There was nothing more pleasurable than good food. Especially when she had to monitor every calorie. But tonight, she'd eat it all. Diet tomorrow, she promised herself.

"Do you get along with your parents?" Logan asked.

Sam chuckled. "Same as you. My parents live in

Florida, so that keeps our relationship on an even keel. When Mom shows up, she's like a force of nature."

"I read you fired her as your manager when you turned eighteen."

"That's correct. I had some grand idea I was an adult and could make my own decisions. I hired a manager who turned out to be a shark. He stole a bunch of money and contracted me to pose nude. I had to hire an attorney to get me out of that mess."

"So no nude photos of you lingering out in the cloud?"

"Heck no. I won't even model lingerie." Sam set her fork down on the salad plate with a clatter.

"My ex-wife was a Victoria's Secret model."

Sam examined Logan's face which had bloomed with color. "I didn't mean . . ."

"No, it's fine. It's one of the reasons we got divorced."

"I get it. Not many men would be comfortable with their wives prancing around in underwear for everyone to drool over."

By the time their main course arrived, the conversation had shifted to Logan's software project.

"I can't give too many details, since I have a nondisclosure agreement with the Department of Defense. But it will give a boost to airport and train security systems."

Sam watched Logan's face become animated as he talked about algorithms and software code. She understood less than a tenth of what he said, but she loved watching his green eyes light up. How had she ever thought he was plain? While not movie star handsome like Dawson Knox, he had a kind of boy-next-door appeal. Kind of like Shia LaBeouf, but with longer hair. And without the beard.

"You stopped listening," Logan said.

Sam's face grew hot. "Sorry. You lost me in the details."

"I didn't mean to bore you. This night is supposed to be about you and your birthday."

"Well, since I've never had a proper birthday party before, I have nothing to compare it to. So far, this is the best birthday I've ever had." She smiled at him, hoping to relieve his discomfort.

By the time dessert arrived, accompanied by tiny cups of cappuccino, Sam was sleepy. She covered her mouth as a yawn worked its way up her throat.

"You look tired," Logan said, his gaze traveling over her face.

"Too much excitement."

Sam dipped a spoon into the creme brulé and took a bite. "Oh. My. Goodness. This is fantastic." She closed her eyes and let the perfection slide across her tongue before she swallowed.

When she opened her eyes, Logan was reaching into his jacket. His had reappeared holding a small black box. Her pulse quickened. If this was going to be a proposal, she'd have to say no.

Too soon, she wanted to shout.

"Happy birthday, Sam," Logan said, opening the box to reveal a pair of ruby earrings. "They're your birthstone," he added.

"They're beautiful," Sam said with a relieved exhale. She pulled the box toward her and lifted it close. Her eyes filled with tears as she gazed at the perfectly cut jewels. "Thank you."

"I hope it isn't too personal," Logan said. "I wasn't sure what to get."

"It's perfect."

Sam ran a finger over the cool stones. How thoughtful of Logan. Her heart sank at the thought of returning to New York and diving back into her career. How could she leave behind the simple pleasures she'd enjoyed while in hiding? She'd found someone who valued the same things she did. Family, true and lasting relationships, with a bit of fun thrown in. When was the last time someone had celebrated her? Not because of what they could gain by being with her. And not because she was some trophy to be photographed. Logan saw her as a normal person.

Once this stalker situation was resolved, she had to make a decision.

Chapter 29

The jet touched down at the Rochester airport at dusk on July 5. He and Sam had spent the day after her birthday strolling around the city of Paris. They'd seen the Arc de Triomphe and had gone to the top of the Eiffel Tower. They'd sampled pastries from a rolling cart and sipped coffee from the smallest to-go cups he'd ever seen.

They'd kissed a few times, but Sam's childlike enthusiasm over sightseeing had overridden his desire. Back in the plane, she'd immediately fallen asleep. Logan watched her sleep, asking himself if he was brave enough to ask her to stay with him for more than a few weeks.

His brain whirled with possible scenarios. One where Sam gave up her modeling career for him. Another where she cut her commitments down to a few per year. His head hurt from trying to imagine his life without Sam and hoping she felt the same.

But what were the chances?

Don't even think about it, Log Jam. He'd tried asking one of the cheerleaders to the prom, but his nemesis, Bruce, had seen him talking to her. *She's so out of your league you can't even lick her shoe.*

How he'd managed to get married was still a mystery. Vivian and he had been a lot alike. She'd been studying chemistry when they met in college. It had been like geek meets nerd when they'd met on campus. As she was two years older than him, Logan had felt he'd won the lottery when she'd glanced his way.

Things had gone south after Vivian had given birth to Mandy. A friend had encouraged her to try out for a modeling show. Even after having a baby, Vivian still had a great shape. The show had given her a makeover and turned Vivian into a beauty.

He was still amazed at how a good haircut and professional makeup could make a plain woman beautiful. Except for Sam. She was gorgeous even without makeup and with her pinking-shears haircut.

Sam stirred when the plan bumped onto the tarmac. "Wake up, sleepyhead," Logan said.

She stretched her arms over her head and raised her seat up. "I didn't realize how tired I was."

They arrived back at Logan's house and Sam immediately went upstairs. "I need a long, hot shower," she said.

"I'll have Carmen bring your bags up."

Sam paused with her hand on the banister. She spoke over her shoulder. "Don't you dare. "That's a man's job."

Logan shook his head and grabbed her bags, lugging them up the stairs.

He found Mandy in her bedroom, clothing spread over her bed.

"How was your time with Ainsley?" he asked.

"It was amazing," Mandy said. She flipped a hand toward the bed. "I got some new clothes. Thanks, Dad." Mandy pulled his debit card from her back pocket and handed it to him with a flourish. "I promise I didn't bankrupt you."

"Glad to hear it."

"How about you? How was Paris? Can I go next time? Ainsley's already been twice."

Logan rubbed a hand over his face. "Sure." He was tired enough to agree to anything.

Mandy squealed and grabbed her phone. "I'm going to text Ainsley."

Logan retreated from Mandy's room and went to his own bedroom. He lay on the bed fully clothed and fell asleep.

When he woke up the next morning, the house was empty. Carmen had left a note on the fridge.

'Dinner needs to warm in the oven for thirty minutes at 350. Salad is made too.'

He found Mandy on the deck, stretched out in the early morning sun, earbuds planted in her ears.

"Where's Sam?"

Sam woke early refreshed from an unbroken night's sleep. She unpacked her bags, took a shower, and dressed in a loose pair of sweats and a long-sleeved T-shirt.

"Where are my sneakers?" She asked, searching again in the closet. They were probably at the rental. She'd run next door and get them while the house was quiet. No doubt if Logan saw her, he'd offer to retrieve them.

He'd done enough for her. Jetting her off to Paris for a birthday celebration, ruby earrings, and an amazing time seeing as many sights as they could squeeze in.

Dew dampened her bare feet as she strode across the berm separating the two houses. Sam gripped the wood rail going up the steps, careful not the slip on the wet wood.

She unlocked the French door and stepped into the house. She found her sneakers tucked under the bed.

Returning downstairs, she set them on the coffee table and went in search of a pair of socks. After searching unsuccessfully through the closet, the bureau drawers and the dirty clothes hamper, she gave up.

The doorbell rang.

"Who could that be?" Sam glanced at her phone. It was a few minutes after eight. She put her eye up to the peephole and saw Frank standing on the porch.

"Frank, what are you doing here?" she asked, swinging open the door.

"Hi, Samantha. Skyler asked me to bring you more mail." He thrust a large white envelope toward her.

"She usually lets me know," Sam said, taking the envelope.

"Oh, yeah. She lost her phone again."

"Figures. She needs to Velcro it to her hand." Sam stepped back and prepared to close the door.

"Do you think I could get some water?"

"Of course." Sam ignored the slight uneasy feeling creeping up her back. This was Frank, photographer extraordinaire. "Come in."

Sam closed the door behind him. "Come into the kitchen, and I'll get you a bottle from the fridge."

Frank followed so close on her heels to the kitchen she could feel his breath on the back of her neck. Goosebumps broke out on her arms. She reached into the refrigerator and grabbed a water bottle. When she turned, she froze.

Frank held a gleaming knife in his hand. "Beautiful Samantha. Don't scream, or I'll be forced to hurt you. And we don't want that, do we?"

Sam shook her head unable to speak. Her heart thudded painfully against her ribcage. She set the water on the counter and took a step back.

"Go into the living room," Frank said, using the knife as a pointer.

Sam did as he said. Frank dragged a chair from the

dining room and positioned it in front of the stone fireplace.

"Sit," he commanded.

Sam measured the distance between her and the door. Could she make it before Frank attacked her from behind? She shifted on the chair, already feeling the knife blade in her back.

Frank pulled zip ties from his pants pocket. He set the knife on the coffee table. "I'm trusting you to sit quietly while I restrain you. If you scream, I will duct tape your mouth. Do you understand?"

Sam nodded. Frank used the zip ties to bind her wrists together. When he finished, he moved to the windows facing the deck and closed all the blinds, plunging the room into semi darkness.

"That's better," he said. "Now your next-door neighbor can't see inside."

Frank picked up the knife again and sat on the edge of the coffee table facing her. "You are so beautiful, Samantha. It's too bad no one will see you after today. But you won't mind, will you? Once your pretty face is marred, no one will want you. No one except me."

Frank's words send a chill through her. "Did you write those letters?"

"You mean you didn't know? I'm disappointed in you, Samantha. I saw the way you looked at me when I took your photos. Always beckoning me with your eyes, your body. We're going to be so happy."

What did he mean, once her face was marred? Did

he plan to cut her to pieces? Hot tears filled her eyes and spilled down her cheeks.

"I hope those are tears of happiness, my darling." Frank moved to wipe her face.

Sam cringed away.

"No, no. Don't do that," Frank warned. "You don't have to play hard to get anymore. Now that we're together, we're going to be so happy."

Bile rose up Sam's throat when Frank stroked her wet cheeks. She forced herself to remain still. If she could find a way to distract him, she could make a run for it.

They both jumped when someone banged on the back door.

"Sam? You in there?"

Sam let out a breath. Logan's voice carried through the glass door.

"Sam?"

Chapter 30

Frank sprang to his feet and paced around the room. Logan banged on the door a couple more times. Sam heard his footsteps clomp down the wood deck stairs. Maybe he'd go back to his house and return with a spare key.

Then what? Would Frank stab him and turn the knife on her?

"Ignore him," Sam said, licking her dry lips.

Frank's eyes held a crazed look. "You should never have kissed him, Samantha. He isn't the one for you." Frank resumed his seat on the coffee table and raised the knife, resting the flat side on her mouth.

"He won't want to kiss you when I'm done."

Sam's body shook with sobs. She squeezed her eyes closed and waited for the sharp blade to cut through her skin.

"Sam?" Mandy's voice called from the front entry. "Sam, are you here?"

Frank stiffened. "Tell her to come in," he

demanded, pressing the knife tip on her cheek.

Sam swallowed. "In here," she called.

Frank rose and waited just inside the door until Mandy entered. He grabbed her arm and shoved her toward the couch.

"Sit."

Mandy's eyes widened when she saw Sam. "What's going on?"

"Shut up. Sit down and be quiet." Frank paced the room, back and forth, muttering to himself.

Sam sent what she hoped was an encouraging smile in Mandy's direction. Mandy's eyes were the size of dinner plates.

My dad is coming. Mandy mouthed the words. Sam gave her head a quick shake. *No.* The last thing she needed was for Logan to get caught in Frank's madness too.

"Frank, everything will be fine. You and I can leave together, and Mandy will go home. Isn't that right, Mandy?"

Frank whirled and strode to where Sam sat. "This isn't how I had it planned."

Sam tried to keep her voice soothing, though she wanted to scream for help. "Let's just go, Frank. It'll be fine."

Frank stroked Sam's hair. She tried not to gag. "You shouldn't have cut your hair, Samantha. You're going to let it grow, aren't you? When we get to my place, we'll get rid of that blue color, and you'll go back to blonde. My Samantha is so beautiful, isn't she?" Frank glanced to Mandy. "Isn't she?" he said, his voice raised.

"Yes. Sam is beautiful." Mandy's voice shook.

"Her name is Samantha."

Mandy looked ready to cry. Sam hoped Mandy would run for the door when she could distract Frank.

"Where are we going, Frank?" Sam asked.

"You'll see. It will be perfect. I have it all ready for you."

Sam sent Mandy a hard stare, hoping the girl could suddenly read her mind. But Mandy sat frozen in place, terrified to move an inch.

Frank resumed his pacing. When he wasn't looking in her direction, Sam mouthed the word *Run*. Mandy glanced at Frank and back at Sam. Sam nodded once.

Mandy shot to her feet and bolted for the hall leading to the front door. Frank moved to stop her, but she was quick. Probably from all the running she'd done in lacrosse.

Not a nanosecond later, Logan ran into the room holding a wicked-looking gun. "Don't move!" he shouted.

Logan stood in the open front door long enough to hear the male voice telling his daughter to shut up. He dashed back home and grabbed his gun from the safe in his bedroom.

He returned to the rental and crept through the front door as Mandy dashed past him.

"Call 9-1-1," he said in a low voice.

When Mandy ran to their house, Logan burst into the living room holding his gun.

"Don't move!"

Logan glanced from Sam to the guy holding a knife and back at Sam. "Are you okay?" he asked. Sam nodded. "Good."

Now what should he do? Hold this guy at gunpoint until the police showed up? He didn't dare take his eyes off the guy, not even to release Sam from the zip ties.

"Put down the knife."

The knife clattered onto the coffee table.

"Put your hands up," Logan said.

They were frozen as if in a tableau. Logan moved closer to where Sam sat. Her face had regained some of its color, but he saw traces of dried tears on her cheeks.

"Are you okay?" he asked again.

"I'm okay," Sam said with a huge exhale.

"Who is this guy?" Logan asked, waving the gun in the man's direction.

"That's Frank."

Frank shifted from one foot to the other and muttered to himself.

"Is he your stalker?"

Sam nodded.

Time seemed to slow down while Logan pointed the gun at the man responsible for terrorizing Sam. He sagged in relief at the sound of approaching sirens. At last.

Moments later, police surged through the front door and filled the living room.

"Drop the gun!" someone shouted.

"I'm not the dangerous one," Logan said.

"Drop the gun now."

Logan carefully placed the weapon on the coffee table and raised his hands. "He's the one you should be arresting," Logan said, pointing toward Frank.

"We'll figure that out down at the station," one uniformed officer said.

"Can someone cut these ties?" Sam asked, raising her hands.

Logan tried to remain calm while he and Frank were handcuffed. Another officer pulled a knife from his pocket and sliced through the plastic ties on Sam's wrists. She rubbed her hands over the red chafe marks.

"Let's go," an officer said, pulling Logan by the arm toward the front door.

"Wait," Samantha said, getting to her feet. She swayed a little and grabbed the back of the chair for support. She pointed at him. "He's Logan Walters. He owns this house." She pointed to Frank. "He's the one you should be arresting."

"Ma'am, we'll sort this all out down at the station. Feel free to follow us there in your own vehicle. These two will be riding with us."

Logan let himself be dragged outside and helped

into the back of a patrol car. Blue and red lights reflected on the faces of the neighbors who'd come out to see the commotion. Logan was beyond humiliated.

Mandy stood at the end of the driveway with her phone held aloft, most likely recording everything. Sam followed, and Logan saw her speaking to one of the police. He gave a curt nod and walked over to where Logan sat, shackled like a common criminal.

The officer opened the patrol car and let Sam lean down to speak to him.

"Can I use your car? I have to go to the station and make a statement, but I don't have a vehicle." Logan was glad to see her face had regained some color.

"Of course. Mandy will get the keys. And please, don't let her come with you."

"You can't stop me, Dad!" Mandy shouted.

Logan grimaced. The only thing that would make this situation worse was if anyone at the police department recognized him.

Chapter 31

Logan was taken to an empty room and shoved onto a hard metal chair.

"How long will this take?"

The officer didn't answer. He closed the door behind him. Sweat broke out between Logan's shoulder blades. He'd done nothing wrong. That crazy guy, Frank, was the one they should lock up.

Logan consulted his watch. He'd give them ten minutes before he started yelling.

Nine minutes and thirty seconds later, the door opened and a man wearing a suit stepped into the room. Logan stared up at him.

"Well, well," the guy said. "I never pictured you as someone I'd see here."

Logan wracked his brain for some memory of who this guy was.

He pulled out a chair and sat across from Logan with a smirk. "Don't remember me, Log Jam?"

It all came crashing back. Bruce Bronson, high

school bully. Logan squirmed on the chair.

"This is all a mistake," Logan said. "A misunderstanding."

"I'm sure." Bruce didn't look convinced. He leaned back and focused an amused glance at Logan. "Why don't you start from the beginning."

Logan exhaled. "Sam—"

"That would be Samantha Jensen, correct?"

"Yes. Samantha and I—"

"I find it hard to believe that you are in any kind of relationship with Samantha Jensen."

"Excuse me?" This was getting out of control.

Bruce pointed a sausage-like finger in Logan's direction. "You, dating a supermodel? Give me a break."

Logan pressed his lips together.

"Nothing to say, Log Jam?"

"I want my attorney."

Bruce glared at him. "Fine. But you aren't under arrest. So you might as well talk. It may be hours before we can get to a phone to call your attorney."

"If I'm not under arrest, then take these handcuffs off me."

Bruce leaned across the table and shoved a key into the locking mechanism. Logan rubbed each of his wrists.

"Samantha Jensen, Sam, has been stalked for several weeks. A few days ago, she received a couple of letters, indicating the stalker was escalating his attempts to get to her. I invited her and her sister, Lauren—"

"The one who's engaged to the billionaire, Paul Montrose?"

"Yes. I invited them to stay at my place. With my daughter," he added, hoping to forestall any inappropriate comment. "Sam went back to my rental this morning. I have no idea why. Apparently, this guy, Frank something, showed up, zip-tied her, and threatened her with a knife. When my daughter went to check on her, she found Frank holding Sam hostage with the knife. My daughter managed to run away, and I held him at gunpoint until your guys showed up."

"Where did you get the gun?"

"Off the internet."

"Is it registered?"

"It isn't a real gun. It's an air gun and doesn't require a permit."

Bruce regarded him with pursed lips. "How did you know to retrieve your gun?"

"When my daughter didn't return after going to check on Sam, I got worried."

"What's your daughter's name? How old is she?"

"Mandy, Amanda, is fourteen. I went to the house and found the front door open. I head Frank yell at my daughter, so I went back to my house and got my gun. Out of my safe."

Bruce pushed his chair back. "I'm going to see if your story checks out. We're questioning Ms. Jensen now."

"When can I leave?" Panic sat like a fifty-pound weight on his chest.

Logan observed Bruce's face change from hard angles to a tiny bit of softness. "Tiffany said you'd changed. She mentioned how helpful you've been with the class reunion, including a generous financial donation."

"High school was a long time ago." Apparently not long enough for some people.

"Yeah." Bruce strode to the door and pulled it open. "Give me a few minutes." He left the door open.

Sam tried to convince Mandy to stay home, but the girl insisted she was going with Sam to the police department.

"I know where Dad's car keys are. If you don't let me go with you, I won't tell you where the keys are."

Sam finally relented, hoping Logan would forgive her. She put the address into the car's GPS.

"It's been a while since I've driven," Sam said, looking over the myriad of controls. Thank goodness her dad had taught her to drive on a stick shift.

"Better not wreck my dad's car," Mandy warned.

Sam grimaced and backed out of the garage. They arrived at the police station a few minutes later.

"You sure you want to come in?" Sam asked, hoping to forestall a blowup when Logan saw them.

"It's *my* dad," Mandy said, climbing out of the car.

A uniformed officer greeted them at the door. "Thanks for coming, Ms. Jensen. Follow me." He led them to a cramped office. "Please have a seat. Detective Bronson will be with you shortly."

Sam and Mandy sat in matching wood chairs facing the scarred wooden desk. She wiped sweaty hands down her capris. She shuddered, remembering how close she'd come to having her face sliced by Frank.

"Are you okay?" Mandy asked.

Sam nodded. But she wasn't okay and wouldn't be for a long time.

A seemingly eternity passed before footsteps sounded in the hall, and a man strode into the room. He wore a dark suit, and Sam guessed him to be mid-thirties. His hair was cut military short. He was once probably handsome, but he'd grown soft with age, and his face was round and chubby.

"Thank you for coming in, Ms. Jensen."

As if she had a choice.

"I'm Detective Bronson. I'd like you to tell me what happened today." He extended his hands on the desk and clasped them together.

Sam sucked in a breath. After today, she never wanted to think about Frank again.

"I've been renting a house here on the lake."

"Vacation?"

"No. I've gotten some weird letters from a stalker."

"Did you report them?"

Was this guy going to interrupt her every time she

opened her mouth?

"I did. The police in New York City said they were investigating." Sam used air quotes. This seemed to annoy the detective.

"Go on."

"My manager thought it would be a good idea for me to get away for a while." She waited, but this time he let her continue. "I rented the house Logan owns."

"Logan Walters?"

"Yes. He lives next door."

"That's my dad," Mandy piped up.

"Right. So anyway, a couple of days ago …" Had it only been a couple of days? So much had happened. Her birthday, Paris, deepening their relationship. "I got two more letters. Logan thought it would be better for me to get out of the house."

"The photos. Tell him about the photos," Mandy said.

"Photos?" The detective spread his hands on the desk.

Sam glanced at Mandy. "Right. There were a bunch of pictures of me at the house and on the lake that went out on the internet."

"Is that unusual? I would think you'd be used to being the target of reporters and such."

Did his voice have a drop of disdain? Sam mentally rolled her eyes. People had no idea what it was like to constantly be in the spotlight.

"I was supposed to be in hiding, remember? The

pictures were taken without my knowledge." Sam swallowed against her suddenly dry mouth. She'd gone back to the rental for something.

"Could I have some water?"

The detective rolled his chair back and left. He returned a few minutes later with two lukewarm bottles of water. Sam cracked hers open and drank deeply.

"Let's talk about what happened when you were at the house."

Sam closed her eyes. "I woke early. There was something I left at the rental. I can't remember what." She opened her eyes with a flood of panic. "Why can't I remember?" She started to shake, huge shudders as she flashed back to the knife against her lips.

Mandy laid a hand on her arm. "It's okay, Sam. You're safe now."

Sam sucked in a shuddering breath. Tears filled her eyes. "I'm sorry. I need a moment."

"We have time." The detective reached behind him for a box of tissues. He shoved the box across the desk. Mandy yanked a few tissues and forced them into Sam's clutched fist.

Sam thrust aside the memory and focused on the chain of events. "I was at the house. The doorbell rang." Sam hugged her arms across her chest and rocked back and forth. "Frank was ..."

Why had she let him come in? She'd ignored the prickle of unease and opened the door anyway. Just like that photographer when she was sixteen. Instead of going with her mom to get something to drink, she'd stayed, ignoring the way he'd stared. While her mom was out of the studio, he'd reached under her dress, grabbing and probing. When he forced his mouth on hers, she'd threatened to scream. He'd laughed. *Laughed.* Said her career would be over if she said anything.

She'd felt violated. Ashamed she'd somehow been at fault. She'd never told anyone.

Maybe this thing with Frank was her fault, too. Had she given him signals she was interested in him?

"Please continue." The detective's voice cut into her runaway thoughts.

Sam took another sip of water, noticing her shaking hands. She set the bottle on the desk clasped her hands together in her lap.

"Frank said he was there to bring my mail."

"Is that a usual thing?"

"He said Skyler, that's my manager, sent him. He'd brought my mail once before." Sam tried to keep her voice from quavering as she told how Frank had forced her into the chair and zip-tied her wrists together. "He said he was going to cut my face." Tears pooled in her eyes and dripped down her cheeks.

Mandy reached over and squeezed her arm around Sam's shoulder.

The detective remained silent while Sam composed herself. She sucked in a breath and continued. "Anyway, he kept saying I was going to be his. We would go away together. Stuff like that. Mandy came in, and he made her sit on the couch. She ran, and then, Logan showed up."

Sam shot to her feet. "I'm done now. I want to leave."

Chapter 32

Logan crossed one leg over the other and tapped his fingers on the scratched metal table. He'd been waiting fifteen minutes and was ready to leave. If he wasn't under arrest, he could walk out the door.

Which he did. Logan glanced down the hall outside the interrogation room. To his right, the hall dead-ended with a door. He headed left.

His speed increased when he spied Sam and Mandy exiting an office ahead.

"Sam!"

She whirled, saw him, and rushed to him. Logan gathered her in his arms. She clung to him, sobs wracking her body.

"Are you okay?" What a dumb question. Of course she wasn't okay. She was wetting the front of his shirt and crying. "Mandy? Why are you here. I told you to stay home."

Mandy glared at him. "Sam needed me."

Logan lifted the side of his mouth in a smile. He

reached out and pulled her into their group hug. "Of course. I'm sorry."

Bruce Bronson stood in the doorway to an office, hands on his hips. "We're not finished."

Logan looked him in the eye. They weren't in high school anymore, and he wasn't that scared kid, locked in the janitor's closet. "Yes, we are. If you have any more questions, you can call my assistant and set an appointment."

Logan moved Sam under one arm and headed toward the door. "I'm not the bad guy here," he said over his shoulder. "Frank is the one you should be questioning."

He herded Sam and Mandy out in the summer sunshine. Taking a breath of fresh air, Logan felt the stress release from his body. "Let's go home."

Home. The word never sounded so good. Sam relaxed into Logan's side. She couldn't imagine anyplace she'd rather be.

Logan pulled into the garage at his house. Before she could open the door, Logan laid a hand on her thigh.

"Mandy, could you go on into the house? I want to talk to Sam alone for a moment."

For once, Mandy didn't argue or complain. She hopped out of the car. Sam watched her stride into the house. Sam turned expectantly toward Logan.

"I want you to know you can stay at my place for as long as you want. If you're uncomfortable being there, I'll leave. Or make arrangements for you to go somewhere else."

Sam inhaled with a shaky breath. "I don't know what I want right now. Except I'd love a cup of coffee and a soft fluffy pillow."

"You've got it."

Sam opened the door and stepped into the garage. She glanced toward the rental and shuddered. Logan stepped up beside her and grasped her hand. She welcomed the warmth of his palm against hers.

"Thanks for being there. For rescuing me."

Logan smiled. "Any time."

Sam suppressed another shudder. "Let's hope it never happens again."

In the house, Logan shoved her gently toward the living room. "Go relax, and I'll bring you some coffee."

Sam heard him talking with Carmen, but she couldn't make out the words. She pulled out her phone and sent a text to Skyler. **Call me.**

Her phone rang as Logan handed her a steaming cup of coffee with just the right amount of cream. He inclined his head toward the sliding glass door and mouthed, 'I'll be outside.'

Sam nodded and answered the phone.

"You will never believe what happened," Sam said to Skyler

"I saw the headline on Buzz Feed. Are you okay?"

Sam blew out a breath through pursed lips. "I am now."

"Start from the beginning," Skyler demanded.

Sam gave her an abbreviated version of what happened, leaving out the scary part where Frank threatened to disfigure her.

They talked for over an hour, discussing Sam's career and upcoming contracts. Sam's gaze returned again and again to where Logan sat on the deck, laptop open and hands poised over the keys. Was he working or only pretending to work?

She finished her conversation with Skyler and carried her empty coffee cup into the kitchen. Carmen turned from the sink and rushed over to embrace her.

"Miss Sam, are you okay?"

Sam spoke against Carmen's soft shoulder. "I am now."

"Mr. Logan was so worried about you when he couldn't find you this morning." She clucked her tongue.

Sam smiled and pulled away. "I know."

"He is a good man, Miss Sam."

"I know," Sam repeated.

She set the cup in the sink and sauntered through the cavernous living room to the back door. She paused a moment to watch Logan through the glass. His head turned to look at the crystal blue waters of Lake Skaneateles, then bowed his head back over the keyboard. He pushed his glasses up his nose.

How had she ever thought Logan dumpy? He was an adorable geek. And her hero. He looked up from his laptop as she slid the door open.

"Finished?" he asked.

Sam pulled in a breath and blew it out. "Yeah." She walked to the rail and leaned her back against it, crossing her legs at her ankles. "Had a good talk with Skyler."

Logan pushed back his chair and came around the table to stand next to her.

"I've made a couple of decision," Sam said. She watched Logan's face to gauge his reaction.

"And?" He clasped her hand, entwining their fingers.

"I'm going to take some time off. Skyler is canceling all my upcoming contracts."

She sent Logan a sideways glance, captivated again by his emerald-colored eyes. "So I was thinking . . . maybe I could, you know, hang around for a little longer?"

Logan appeared to be thinking.

"Maybe see if there are any rentals available in the area?"

A ghost of a smile crossed Logan's face. "I might know of one."

"Yeah, but I heard the landlord is super nosy."

"Hm. Nosy."

"Yeah, like he keeps coming over to check the hot water heater. Stuff like that."

"So how long would you need the rental for?"

Sam glanced up at the house next door. Even though Frank had invaded her space there, she was ready to go back and find out who she was if she wasn't modeling."

"I'm not sure. Do you think the landlord would let me stay until, oh, I don't know, until school starts in the fall?"

"And then what?"

Sam shrugged. "I don't know." She unclasped their hands and turned to face the lake. *Small Fry* bobbed in the wake created by a passing motorboat. "I don't know how to do anything except pose in front of a camera. I can't cook, I don't know how to do laundry, and I'm basically useless."

"You aren't useless to me." Logan pulled her to his chest and wrapped his arms around her. "Stay as long as you want."

"But—"

"No buts. I'll head back to the City when Mandy has to go back to school. You still have an apartment there, right?"

Sam nodded against his shoulder.

"Let's take it one day at a time until then, okay?"

"Okay."

Chapter 33

Later that day after a long nap, Sam told Logan she was ready to move back into his rental.

"Are you sure?" Logan's face clouded with concern.

"I'm sure. But will you go with me?"

"Of course."

Sam packed her clothes and gathered her cosmetics from the bathroom. After a last glance around to be sure she'd gotten everything, she schlepped the bags down the stairs. She lingered on the bottom step, second-guessing her decision to go back to the rental.

But she refused to be a victim again. Never again. She'd had a long conversation with Lauren, who'd also questioned the wisdom of going back there.

"I have to figure some things out," Sam had told her. "Like who I am and why I'm doing what I'm doing."

Lauren had reluctantly agreed, but only after insisting she call their parents. The conversation with her mother had gone better than she expected.

When she told her mom she wouldn't be able to send them any money until she was working again, her mom had surprised her with her answer.

"Oh, honey, I haven't used any of that. I've been putting it in a savings account for you."

"I thought—"

"I know, I should have told you sooner. But I figured if you wanted to assuage your guilt over firing me when you turned eighteen, I'd let you. But Dad and I truly don't need your money."

Sam had cried for ten minutes after that call.

"Ready?" Logan reached for her rolling bag and put out a hand for her carry-on.

"I think so. I'm a little nervous."

"Rightly so. My offer still stands. You can stay here."

Sam squared her shoulders. "I need to do this. No more running scared."

"Okay, then. Let's go."

Sam wasn't sure what she expected to find when Logan unlocked the front door of the rental. The house looked the same, except the knife and the gun were gone. Someone had moved the chair where Frank had held her hostage back to the dining room.

She inhaled and blew out the breath through pursed lips. "I'll be fine," she said, speaking to herself more than to Logan.

"I'll put your bags in the bedroom."

Sam walked through the living room and out to the back deck. The lake glittered in the afternoon sunlight. Shrieks of laughter sounded from the diving platform as brave swimmers dove into the chilly water. Life went on. Tragedies happened and life continued.

Logan came out onto the deck and stood beside her. "Want to go for a sail?"

"Maybe later. I think I'm going to chill for a bit."

"Want me to leave you alone?"

Sam sent him a grateful look. "Please."

Logan leaned in and planted a kiss on her cheek. "Until later, then."

Sam watched him stride down the stairs and cross the distance between the two houses. When he reached his deck, he looked up and waved. She waved back.

Sinking onto one of the loungers, Sam closed her eyes and thanked God for bringing Logan into her life.

"Are you sure I can't go next door?" Mandy asked.

"For the fifth time, no. Sam said she wanted to be left alone for a while."

Mandy's shoulder slumped. "But—"

"Later, Mandy. Sam needs to figure some things out."

"Like what?"

Logan stretched his legs out onto the coffee table. Mandy sprawled on the opposite sofa. "Sam had the scare of her life from the stalker. She is taking some time off from her career. She needs to figure out if she will go back to modeling or not."

"What else would she do?"

Logan sighed. "That's what she needs to figure out."

"I'm glad I'm not an adult."

"Me too." Logan had his hands full dealing with Mandy's mercurial moods. What would it be like when she turned eighteen? He shuddered. If he still had custody of Mandy during the next four years, he'd have to figure out a way to guide her into a career.

"I think I want to be a model," Mandy said.

"Not going to happen."

Mandy shot to her feet. "When I turn eighteen, I can do whatever I want." She snatched her phone off the sofa and stomped out of the room.

Logan heaved a huge sigh. Maybe Sam could talk her out of pursuing a modeling career. Maybe scare Mandy with the possibility of attracting a stalker.

No, that wasn't a good idea. Once his daughter became an adult, she'd do what she wanted. Until then, he'd latch onto the lifeboat and hope they'd make it safely to shore. With Sam by his side.

Logan stepped onto his deck and stared over the surface of the lake. The open water beckoned him, but he wanted to stay close in case Sam needed him.

He was needed.

Since his divorce, he'd been in a self-imposed safety bubble. Mandy's arrival was the first hole poked in that bubble. Sam had obliterated the remaining wall between him and the outside world. A month ago, Logan wouldn't have believed he'd not only be in a relationship, but helping with his high school class reunion. He'd been out in public more times in the past few weeks than in the past two years.

Logan glanced up at the clouds scuttling across the blue sky and said a quick prayer of thanks. Perhaps it was time to go back to church. He grinned to himself. Now that he had stylish clothes, that is.

Chapter 34

Four weeks later:

"Are you ready to go, Dad?"

Logan stood at the bottom of the staircase and watched his daughter descend. His breath caught at the sight of her in a nice dress with her hair pulled up into a fancy hairdo.

"Do I look all right?" Mandy hesitated when she reached him.

"You look beautiful." And she did.

Mandy's cheeks bloomed with color. "Sam helped me with my hair."

"Are you wearing makeup?" Was fourteen too young?

"Only a little mascara and lip gloss." Mandy swept past him and headed toward the door.

"Come on, Dad. You don't want to be late for your class reunion."

"And you can't be late for your dance."

"You'll pick me up when it's over, right?"

"Absolutely. And you'll stay close to Ainsley the entire night."

Mandy rolled her eyes. "I promise. Daxton will probably be too busy to ask me to dance."

"I'm relieved."

Mandy swatted his arm. "His Hi-Y group has been planning this dance for weeks. I hope a lot of kids turn out."

Logan got Mandy settled into the back seat of his Aston Martin and walked next door. He knocked on the door of his rental, butterflies swarming in his stomach. He and Sam were heading to his class reunion dinner and dance. He smoothed the front of his tuxedo and glanced down to be sure his shoes still shone.

The door opened and Sam stood there with a smile.

"You clean up nice," she said.

Logan's breath caught. Sam wore a pale pink sheath that dropped from her shoulders to just above her knees. She'd removed the blue dye from her hair, and the blonde locks caught the early evening sun. After a professional haircut, the short pixie cut suited her.

"Is something wrong?" Sam asked when Logan remained silent.

"N-no. You look amazing."

A wide smile broke over her face. "Thank you."

Logan held out his hand. Sam grasped it and stepped over the threshold. With her high heels, she towered over him by at least six inches. But it didn't matter. His chest puffed up with pride. She'd chosen him. He couldn't wait to get to the reunion. All those kids who bullied him in high school would have their mouths shut.

Sam surprised herself at how excited she was to go to Logan's class reunion. Such a huge difference from attending a black-tie, red-carpet affair. There'd be no paparazzi waiting to snap a dozen photos. No microphone shoved in her face asking intrusive questions. No having to make vapid conversation with people she barely knew and liked even less.

Since she'd helped on the reunion committee, Tiffany had warmed up and had even invited her to coffee. Small things like coffee with a new friend made her feel normal. That feeling had eluded her since she was fourteen. Life after modeling was rewarding with its normalcy.

They dropped Mandy off at her dance and headed toward the community center.

"Are you nervous?" Sam asked after Logan wiped his hands down his thighs for the third time.

"Yes."

She patted his leg. "It'll be fun."

"I keep thinking about Branson. You know, Tiffany's husband."

"Ancient history. Remember who you are. You are a software engineer with more money than they'll ever see in a lifetime."

"It isn't about the money."

"Isn't it?" Sam turned to observe his profile.

"It's hard to explain. Sometimes, I still feel like that nerdy kid, trying to fit in, whether I have money more not."

"I bet everyone at the reunion feels the same. All of us want to fit in."

They pulled up to the community center. Cars jammed the parking lot, and Logan was forced to circle around looking for an empty spot.

"Want me to drop you off?" he asked, glancing down at her shoes.

"And miss the opportunity to make an entrance with you? I don't think so."

Sam had to admit, she was a little nervous too. Was her designer dress too much for this small-town event? Lots of wealthy people lived on Lake Skaneateles. But would they judge her? Sam was used to being stared at, photographed, and gossiped about. But these were Logan's people. And this was his night.

"Are you sure I look all right?" Sam asked.

"You're nervous?" Logan's voice was incredulous.

Sam giggled. "A little."

"Come on, lady. Let's go make an entrance." Logan got out of the car and walked around to open her door. Sam stepped out and grabbed Logan's arm for support.

Loose pebbles on the asphalt parking lot crunched under their feet as they strolled to the door. A balloon arch in the school's colors sat at the entrance. Inside the building, a few alumni sat at a table handing out name tags and checking people in.

"There you are!" Tiffany's voice rang out above the noise. She strode up to Sam and gave her a quick hug. "I'm so glad you made it." She turned and pulled Logan into a hug.

Sam hid her amusement when Logan kept his arms down at his sides.

"The room looks beautiful," Sam said, following Tiffany into the event center.

"I can't thank you enough for your help. Both of you." Tiffany's glance took in her and Logan.

"Our pleasure," Sam said. She glanced around, proud of the way the room turned out. Silk palm trees stood like sentinels against the walls. The wood backdrop she and Logan had helped paint had attracted several people, commenting on which car they'd owned during their high school years.

Sam glanced at Logan. His face was set, and a muscle clenched and unclenched in his jaw.

"You're doing great," she said. "Relax."

"Let's find our table." Logan pulled her around the room until they found their names on the place cards on one of the tables. Two other couples had already taken their places.

Logan pulled her chair out and waited for her to sit before taking his place.

"Hello, everyone. I'm Sam. Logan's date."

They went around the table and introduced themselves. Sam worked to cover Logan's awkwardness by asking, "Which of you are alumni?"

One of the women pointed to her name tag. "The ones with the stars indicate who's an alumnus."

"Oh, I didn't realize," Sam said, looking down at her own name tag. "That's convenient."

"So, Logan, what do you do for work," asked one of the men with a star on his name tag.

He cleared his throat. Sam held his hand under the table. "I do some work for the Department of Defense."

"No kidding. So do I."

They began a discussion about software, hardware, and stuff that held no interest for Sam. She leaned toward the plump woman sitting closest to her. Her name tag read 'Robin.'

"Did you know Logan in high school?" Sam asked.

"Not really," Robin said. "I was with the theater crowd. We really didn't cross paths. What about you? Where did you go to school?"

"Hornell." No use in elaborating about her unusual high school experience.

"How long have you and Logan been together?"

Sam glanced at Logan to see if he was paying attention. But he was still engrossed in conversation with the guy next to him. "A month or so. We met when I rented his house on the lake."

"I always thought he was cute," Robin said. "But shy."

Sam smiled. "He is shy." She squeezed his thigh. "But not once you get to know him."

"What do you do for work?" Robin asked.

Sam had a moment of panic. How to answer that question? "Oh, I'm, uh, taking a break right now."

Robin's face flamed. "Oh, I'm sorry. You're the model Tiffany was telling me about. I heard about that stalker. How awful for you."

"Is everyone having a good time?" Tiffany's shrill voice interrupted the flow of conversation around the table. She must have stopped at the no host bar before coming to their table. She wobbled a bit on her Prada heels.

"Logan, would you get me something to drink?" Sam asked, nudging his shoulder. "White wine."

He pushed his chair back and gave Sam a questioning look. Sam patted his vacant seat.

"Have a seat, Tiffany."

"I see you've met Robin," Tiffany said, leaning into Sam's side.

"Yes, I have."

Chapter 35

Logan made his way around the tables and reached the bar. A few guys huddled around the bar, sipping beers. A cursory glance showed their name tags lacked the star. Good. He wouldn't have to make nice with fellow alumni.

"White wine, please," he said to the bartender.

A couple of the men filtered away. Logan watched them return to their dates at the tables. Dinner plates appeared on the tables, served by wait staff.

"Here you go, sir," the bartender said, setting the glass of wine on the bar. "Anything else?"

"No, thanks." Logan pulled a bill from his pocket and stuffed it into the tip jar.

"You one of the popular kids?" Logan turned to see who addressed him.

A heavyset man wearing a too-tight sport coat leaned against the end of the bar, nursing a cocktail.

"Hardly," Logan said.

"You're that software guy, aren't you?"

Logan's glance shifted from the man to his table. Sam seemed engrossed in conversation with Tiffany. With a sigh, he turned to the man.

"I'm not sure what you mean."

The man stuck out a hand to shake Logan's. "I'm Marshall Gaines. I saw the write-up about you in the *Financial Times* a few months back. You sold that facial recognition software to the government."

Was there a question hiding in there?

"Yes." He shook the man's hand. "Logan Walters."

"Very impressive. I'm working on a program to detect micro expressions on travelers boarding international flights. Very hush-hush stuff. Kind of like what you're doing."

This guy seemed to know a lot about Logan's business. Sweat prickled his armpits. He glanced again at his table, hoping to excuse himself from this awkward conversation.

"I'm not trying to get up in your business," Marshall said. "But I wonder if you'd be willing to compare notes on our respective software. Might be a way to work together and not only make a pile of money but help keep terrorists from invading our country."

Logan didn't need money, but this guy didn't know that. Apparently, he hadn't read the entire article in the *Financial Times* that he'd sold his program for close to a billion dollars in cash and stock options.

"I'll let you know," Logan said.

Marshall thrust a business card at him. "Here's my card. Give me a call."

Logan nodded, picked up the glass of wine and strode away from the bar. When he reached the table, Tiffany glanced up.

"I guess that's my cue to leave," she said, rising to her feet. "Dancing will start as soon as the dinner plates are cleared."

Logan watched her sway to the next table. He set the wine in front of Sam and sank into the chair.

"Who was that?" Sam asked when Logan returned to the table.

"I'll tell you later."

Once Logan was engaged in conversation with the man next to him, she turned back to Robin, who stared at Tiffany's back as she stopped to talk to another group.

"I can't stand her," Robin said, turning her gaze back to Sam.

"Tiffany? Why not?"

Robin made a face. "She thinks she's better than everyone else."

Sam frowned. "I don't think that's true."

"You don't know her."

Sam rose to the defense of her new friend. "I've gotten to know her recently. Tiffany wants the same thing we all want—acceptance."

Robin's mouth turned down. "If you say so."

Time to change the subject. "What do you do for work?" Sam asked.

"I work for a group home for teenage girls. We take in girls who either can't function in a foster home environment or who've been repeatedly kicked out of foster care."

"Sounds fulfilling."

"It is equally fulfilling and depressing. Some of our girls age out of the foster system and become homeless or get involved in human trafficking. It's sad. We try to give them all the life skills, but some come to us so broken they don't have a chance."

Sam thought back to her unusual upbringing and thanked God for her parents.

Robin continued. "Would you consider coming to speak to our girls? We have ten young women at the moment. They could use a good female role model."

Sam's breath caught. "What would I talk about?"

"You can show them how to be proud to be a woman. Too many of our girls have been sexually molested by a male relative or even a foster brother. They suffer from gender dysphoria and frankly, they dress like homeless men." Robin gave a lopsided smile.

"I don't know. I'd have to think about it."

"Please do." Robin reached into her purse and pulled out her phone. "Put your contact info in here, and let's touch base."

"Is that a Dior handbag?" Sam asked, pointing

toward Robin's purse.

She laughed. "Oh, no. It's a knockoff. I could never afford the real thing on my salary."

Sam felt her face grow hot. She was used to women bragging about their shoes, clothes, and purses. Name dropping all over the place. She shoved her Hermes bag firmly under the table with one foot.

Sam put her information into Robin's phone. Robin sent her a text. "Now you have my information. Please, do think about it."

The thought of speaking to a group of teenagers struck fear into Sam's heart. Standing in front of a horde of photographers didn't have the same effect as thinking about hostile teen girls. She'd rather face a firing squad.

After they'd finished eating, Sam was ready to leave. She nudged Logan. "Want to go home?" she whispered.

"One dance," he said.

The band began a slow ballad. Logan stood and held out his hand. "May I have this dance?"

Chapter 36

Logan led Sam to the handkerchief-sized dance floor. "I'm not a great dancer," he said.

"Neither am I."

Sam smiled into his eyes and Logan's breath caught. "You are beautiful."

"You are a flatterer, Mr. Walters."

Logan glanced around to see if anyone was smirking at their height difference.

"Stop doing that," Sam said. "I know you're worried that I'm taller than you."

Logan shrugged. "I can't help it."

"Everyone here is more focused on themselves than on us. Just relax, okay?"

How could he relax when all he wanted was to pull Sam out of the room and kiss her senseless? He never felt this way with Vivian. This was the real thing, and Logan was out of his element. What if Sam didn't feel the same way? They'd agreed to take it one day at a time, but Logan was impatient. He wanted a commitment now. Tonight.

"I need to tell you something."

"Okay."

"Not here. Let's leave."

Sam's face clouded. "Aren't you having a good time?"

He wasn't. He was done with talking, done with random guys approaching him at the bar, done with this uncomfortable tuxedo bunching at his waist.

The song ended, and Logan pulled Sam off the dance floor. His brain clogged with the words he wanted to say to Sam. This place wasn't private enough.

Logan groaned with frustration when Sam wanted to stop and tell Tiffany goodbye. Bruce pulled him aside while the women chatted.

"No hard feelings, eh, Logan?" Bruce stuck out his hand to shake Logan's.

Logan forced himself to look Bruce in the eye as their hands met. "No hard feelings."

Bruce exhaled and dropped Logan's hand. "Sorry I was a jerk at the station. I let my jealousy get the better of me."

Logan's head spun. "Jealousy?"

Bruce's mouth held a wry smile. "Yeah, I know. Sounds stupid now. You were always the smart one. Good grades and all. I struggled to land a B."

Logan snorted. "But—"

"I know, I know. I was a dumb jock. And I'm sorry

about the janitor closet thing."

"Uh, okay." Logan's brain refused to make sense of Bruce's words.

"The thing is, if my wife and your girlfriend continue their friendship, we'll be forced together at some point. Know what I mean?"

Logan found himself incapable of more than one-word responses. "Yeah."

Bruce clapped him on the back. "Great. See ya around." Bruce headed toward a group of men clustered at the bar.

Logan was still speechless when Sam pulled on his arm. "Ready to go?"

"Yes." He hustled Sam to his car, careful to steady her. "Those heels must be difficult to walk in."

"I'm used to them. But I'm getting a lot more comfortable in a pair of flip flops, that's for sure."

Sam chattered about her conversation with someone named Robin on the drive back to his house. Logan let her words wash over him as he pondered what he would say when they were home.

Sam slipped off her shoes when he pulled into his driveway. "What did you want to tell me? Back there at the reunion, you said you wanted to tell me something."

Logan sucked in a lungful of air and blew it out. "Not here. Go change your clothes, and let's take the boat out?"

"A nighttime sailboat ride? Sounds romantic." Sam sent a smile his way.

"Wear a sweatshirt."

He climbed out of the car, already sweating with nerves. He opened the passenger door. Sam slid out, her sandals dangling from one finger.

"See you in a few," she said.

Logan watched her cross his driveway to the rental. "Want me to go with you?" he called. "Make sure it's safe?"

"I'm fine." Sam blew him a kiss and unlocked the front door. Logan waited until she was safe inside before loosening his tie and unlocking his own front door.

His phone buzzed with a text.

Mandy: I'm going to stay and help clean up. Daxton will bring me home.

Logan typed out a text telling her in no uncertain terms that she was not allowed to ride with a sixteen-year-old. Before he could hit Send, she sent a follow up text.

Mandy: Ainsley will be with us.

Logan deleted his text and sent a thumbs up emoji instead. It was a good thing Mandy had a ride home. In his haste to get Sam by himself, he'd forgotten he was supposed to pick his daughter up after the dance. Mentally slapping himself on the forehead, he stripped off the tuxedo and changed into a pair of sweats and a tee shirt. He pulled a hoodie on and headed out to the deck to wait for Sam.

What was Logan's big announcement? Sam mulled over the possibilities while she slipped out of the cocktail dress and into a pair of baggy sweats. She added a couple of layers before pulling a hoodie over her head.

Her pulse quickened with anticipation as she prepared to set sail on *Small Fry* with Logan. The full moon hung high in the night sky, its silvery glow casting an ethereal sheen across the surface of the lake. The water shimmered like a vast canvas painted in shades of sepia and silver, each ripple catching the moonlight and dancing with a gentle, mesmerizing grace.

Logan waited on the deck beside his boat. He turned and smiled as she approached.

"Ready?" he asked, holding out a hand to help her board.

"Ready." Sam was ready to go anywhere this man wanted to take her. Paris? Yes. Night sailing on Lake Skaneateles? Oh, yes.

Logan deftly unfurled the sails and let the evening breeze pull them gently across the lake. Sam joined him when he sat in the captain's chair facing the stern.

"It's beautiful out here," she commented.

"Yes, it is. It's the only place I feel free."

"Freedom. It's a wonderful feeling."

Logan inhaled and blew out a breath. "Did you have

fun tonight?"

"I did. Did you?"

Logan shrugged. "It was okay."

"Just okay?" she prodded.

Logan's gaze was on the distant shore. "The thing is, I am uncomfortable around crowds. Even more than two people makes me sweat."

"That's okay, Logan. I get it."

"I want you to understand—"

Sam laid a hand on his arm. "I do. Understand. You have … quirks."

"It's more than a quirk. It's a diagnosis."

"I don't care." And she didn't. Who could honestly say what 'normal' was, anyway?

Logan licked his lips. "I want to have a relationship with you, Samantha Jensen. A long-term one." He sent a quick glance her way before his gaze returned to the dark surface of the lake.

Sam crossed her arms and hugged herself. Isn't that what she wanted to hear? Doubts crept in. "I need to figure some things out," she said after a long pause.

"I want to help you. To be there while you figure things out."

"What about Mandy? Is she ready for you to have a relationship with someone?"

Logan's posture relaxed. "She adores you, Sam."

"But I'm less than ten years older than she is."

Logan turned and placed his hands on her shoulders. "That doesn't matter to her. Or to me. Can you see yourself with someone like me?”

Sam put a finger on his lips. “I would be honored to be with someone like you.”

Logan's next words caught Samantha by surprise. “As my wife?”

Chapter 37

Logan regretted the words as soon as he uttered them. They hung in the air with only the soft background sounds of the lake. Sam's eyes were pools of emotion.

He should have waited. At least for another decade.

Logan's heart beat against his ribs while he waited for Sam's response.

"Yes," she finally said.

"Yes?" Logan couldn't believe his ears.

Sam laid her head on his shoulder. "Yes to you helping me figure out my messed-up life. Yes to helping you with Mandy." She leaned back and stared into his eyes.

"And yes to being your wife. But not quite yet."

Hope rose in his chest. "When?"

Sam sighed. "At least not until my sister gets married. I don't want anything to steal the attention from her."

"When is she getting married? We can plan for the

weekend after."

Sam rolled her eyes. "Relax, Mr. Walters. All in good time. In the meantime, I need a kiss."

Logan was more than happy to oblige.

THE END

Did you read Billionaire and the Baker?

After a career in banking, Jane Daly is living her dream of traveling the United States in her motor home. She's the author of two nonfiction books and The Girl in the Cardboard Box. She's written numerous articles and blogs, but her heart is in creating stories about women facing difficult and even impossible circumstances, emerging scarred but triumphant.

When she's not hunched over her computer, she can be found making new friends in whichever state she finds herself.

9 781965 352816